BEAVER TOWERS

THE SERIES

*F*ar away, on a magical island, is a castle called
Beaver Towers. It was once the home of happy
beavers – until they were betrayed by magic. Magic
which called up evil creatures from the world of
shadows. The animals of the island send out a call for
help and Philip, an ordinary boy, finds himself drawn into
the struggle to save them from the powers of darkness.

There are four exciting books in the *Beaver Towers*
series. Here they are in reading order:

Beaver Towers
The Witch's Revenge
The Dangerous Journey
The Dark Dream

Nigel Hinton was
born in London. He has written
fifteen novels, including four prize-
winners, and a number of scripts for TV and
the cinema. He enjoys swimming, walking, films,
reading, watching football and listening to music,
especially 50s rock 'n' roll and Bob Dylan

Some other books by Nigel Hinton

THE FINDERS

For older readers

BUDDY
BUDDY'S SONG
BUDDY'S BLUES

COLLISION COURSE
OUT OF THE DARKNESS

NIGEL HINTON

THE DARK DREAM

THE FOURTH BOOK IN THE BEAVER TOWERS SERIES

Illustrated by Anne Sharp

PUFFIN BOOKS

For Joey

PUFFIN BOOKS

Published by the Penguin Group
Penguin Books Ltd, 80 Strand, London WC2R 0RL, England
Penguin Putnam Inc., 375 Hudson Street, New York, New York 10014, USA
Penguin Books Australia Ltd, 250 Camberwell Road, Camberwell, Victoria 3124, Australia
Penguin Books Canada Ltd, 10 Alcorn Avenue, Toronto, Ontario, Canada M4V 3B2
Penguin Books India (P) Ltd, 11 Community Centre, Panchsheel Park, New Delhi – 110 017, India
Penguin Books (NZ) Ltd, Cnr Rosedale and Airborne Roads, Albany, Auckland, New Zealand
Penguin Books (South Africa) (Pty) Ltd, 24 Sturdee Avenue, Rosebank 2196, South Africa

Penguin Books Ltd, Registered Offices: 80 Strand, London WC2R 0RL, England

www.penguin.com

Published in Puffin Books 1997

025

Set in 11/14 pt Monophoto Ehrhardt by Rowland Phototypesetting Ltd, Bury St Edmunds, Suffolk

Printed and bound in Great Britain by Clays Ltd, Elcograf S.p.A.

British Library Cataloguing in Publication Data
A CIP catalogue record for this book is available from the British Library

ISBN-13: 978-0-14-038389-8

www.greenpenguin.co.uk

MIX
Paper from
responsible sources
FSC™ C018179

Penguin Books is committed to a sustainable
future for our business, our readers and our planet.
This book is made from Forest Stewardship
Council™ certified paper.

WELCOME TO BEAVER TOWERS
ARE YOU READY FOR ADVENTURE?

If you are, then follow the journey made by a young boy called Philip in the book *Beaver Towers*. He was flying his kite in a park when suddenly he was lifted into the air and carried away.

Follow him – high in the sky, over the mountains, over the sea and far, far away from home . . .

He landed on an island where a terrible witch, Oyin, was capturing all the animals and locking them up in the castle called Beaver Towers. Philip soon became friends with the animals who were still free – a little beaver called Baby B, and his grandfather called Mr Edgar, the kindly Mrs Badger, and three hedgehogs called Mick, Ann and Nick. These hedgehogs look after Doris, an old car, and because of their names everyone calls them The Mechanics.

Philip decided to help them and, after all sorts of dangers, he managed to free the other animals and to defeat Oyin and send her back to her dreadful master, the Prince of Darkness.

The book called *The Witch's Revenge* tells how Oyin was so furious about what Philip had done that she followed him to his home to try to destroy him. Philip was too clever for her, though. He escaped to Beaver Towers and, after many scary adventures, he put an end to the wicked witch for ever.

After that, Philip thought that all his adventures were over. Then, one day, he was amazed to find Baby B and Nick in his house. Mr Edgar had sent them to fetch him back to Beaver Towers. The book *The Dangerous Journey* tells how they made their way back to the island, chased all the way by enemies sent by the Prince of Darkness.

Philip and his friends faced so many dangers and were so brave that they started to develop a wonderful power called think-talking, which allows you to send your thoughts to other people. Mr Edgar was so pleased about this that he decided to take Philip on a journey to meet some special people who could help him increase his powers.

That journey is just about to begin.

Oh, I forgot to tell you something. There isn't just one island – there are two. The second island is a large, bare, round rock not far from Beaver Towers.

It's on that island that our story starts.

Don't go too close, though – there's something horrible lurking there . . .

CHAPTER ONE

In the dim light just before dawn, a dark shape stood on the cliffs of Round Rock Island. It stared across the sea towards another larger island where the castle of Beaver Towers stood. Hatred glowed in the creature's red, serpent eyes and a growl of anger rumbled in its throat.

'Soon you will be mine. And I, the Prince of Darkness, will destroy you.'

At that moment, the first rays of the sun struck the flags flying from the top of the walls of Beaver Towers. The dark shape hid its face and scuttled back into the shadows of a cave.

Philip woke with a start and listened. Had somebody spoken?

There was silence.

Where was he? At home? No. He looked round and remembered.

Oh yes, he was in Baby B's room in Beaver Towers. There was the little beaver curled up in his bed on the other side of the room. Philip smiled at the sight of his sleeping friend. Then he got out of bed and tiptoed over to the window.

The sun was coming up and a new day was beginning. And what an important day! Today he was setting off on a long and mysterious journey with the old beaver, Mr Edgar. Philip felt sad to be leaving all his friends at Beaver Towers but he was excited at the thought of all the adventures in store.

'Come on, Baby B, time to wake up,' Philip said, gently shaking the little beaver's shoulders.

Baby B's eyes opened sleepily, then he blinked and sat up.

'Hello, Flipip,' he yawned. 'Is it morning?'

'Yes, time to get up. Mr Edgar is probably waiting for us.'

Philip dressed quickly but Baby B kept getting the straps on his dungarees buttoned up the wrong way round.

'Oh drat these gungarees!' Baby B said as the straps got tangled up again.

'Let me help,' Philip suggested.

'No thanks. Grandpa Edgar says that I'm bigger enough to do it on my own. Hooray, I did it – look, Flipip!'

Philip didn't have time to say that Baby B had

still got the straps done up the wrong way round because the little beaver was already running out of the room. Philip ran after him.

Baby B bounded down the stairs two at a time then raced along the corridor. At the top of the main staircase he jumped up on to the bannister and started to slide down the rail.

'Wheeee! Look at me, Flipip,' he shouted as he whizzed down.

He was so busy shouting that he forgot to slow down at the bottom. Sergeant Robin was perched on the end of the bannister and the little bird darted into the air as Baby B swept towards him. The beaver shot off the end of the rail, turned a somersault in mid-air and flew towards Mrs Badger who was talking to Mr Edgar in the Great Hall.

'Baby B, look out!' Mrs Badger cried out just before he crashed into her tummy, knocking her flat on her back.

'Thank you for catching me, Mrs Badger,' Baby B said, scrambling off the poor badger. 'I nearly hurted myself.'

'Blow me down, Baby B, you are a scamp,' Mr Edgar said as he helped Mrs Badger to her feet. 'Are you all right, ma'am?'

'Yes, thank you,' Mrs Badger said, rubbing her tummy. 'Just a bit puffed, that's all.'

'I should say you are, ma'am, I should say you are. This madcap grandson of mine came at you like a dratted cannon ball. Really, Baby B, how many times have I told you not to slide down the bannisters?'

'Millions, Grandpa,' Baby B said sheepishly.

'Yes, millions,' the old beaver said, patting his grandson on the head. 'And it's high time you listened and started to grow up.'

'But I *am* growed up. I did doing up my gungarees all by myself this morning, didn't I, Flipip?'

Philip smiled and nodded.

'Hmm, yes . . . well, there's a bit more to being grown up than being able to put on your dungarees,' Mr Edgar said. 'And remember, now that you've learned how to think-talk, I'm relying on you to keep things shipshape at Beaver Towers while I'm away. So you must start acting in a responsible way.'

'Yes, Grandpa,' Baby B said, his eyes growing big and his lower lip starting to tremble. Then he had an idea that seemed to cheer him up. 'It's not just me. Nick can think-talk too. So he can be riskonstable as well, can't he, Grandpa?'

'He most certainly can. The only reason I can go away like this is because I know that you and your young hedgehog friend will be able to get in touch with me just by thinking.'

'Even if you are millions and millions away?' Baby B asked.

'Yes, no matter how far away I am.'

'And will you think-talk to me and Nick, Grandpa?'

A little flicker of sadness passed across Mr Edgar's eyes, then he smiled and shook his head.

''Fraid not, you little rascal. I'm too much of an old duffer nowadays – bit by bit I'm losing all my magic powers. I'll be able to hear you and talk to you when you contact me but I won't be able to contact you. I'll have to rely on young Philip to do that for me. That's why I'm as pleased as Punch that all three of you have learned how to do it. Now come along; I don't know about anybody else, but I'm starving. Time to get some breakfast. We've got a big day ahead.'

CHAPTER TWO

Everybody helped to get the breakfast ready. Mrs Badger set the table while Mr Edgar cut big slices of bread from the loaf that had just finished baking in the oven. Philip fetched the butter and a big bowl of honey, then filled the mugs with fresh, creamy milk.

Baby B's job was to go to the storeroom to get some nuts and apples, but by the time everything else was ready he still hadn't come back. Philip went to look for the little beaver and found him trying to juggle with the apples.

'I can nearly do it – look,' Baby B said, throwing two apples up into the air. The apples fell back down and hit him. 'Ow!' he said, rubbing his head. 'I can nearly do it, 'cept these apples keep being silly.'

Luckily the apples weren't too badly bruised and they made a crisp and juicy end to the delicious breakfast.

'Well,' Mr Edgar said when they all finished eating, 'best to get a move on. Many a mile before midnight, eh lad?'

Philip nodded and stood up. His heart was knocking hard in his chest and he suddenly felt nervous. If only he could stay here in Beaver Towers with Baby B and all the others.

He looked across at Mrs Badger who smiled at him as if she knew what he was feeling. Baby B slipped his paw into Philip's hand and they followed Mr Edgar and Mrs Badger up the stairs, through the Great Hall, and out of the main door.

As they started down the steps, a big cheer went up from all the animals waiting for them in the courtyard. Baby B's parents were there and the little beaver ran down, jumped into his father's arms, and started cheering louder than anyone.

'Blow me down, what a lovely surprise!' Mr Edgar said, beaming with joy. 'Seeing all my friends like this makes me wish I didn't have to go off on this mission. But, as you know, I'm taking Philip to meet some special animals and people. In the meantime, I've left a list of jobs for everyone to do. If there are any problems, Mrs Badger and Mr Stripe are two wise old heads who can sort things out. Just one last word, though – be on your guard! You all remember Oyin, don't you?'

All the animals nodded and a few of them shivered with fear at the memory of the terrible witch who had nearly captured the island.

'Well, the danger is never over. The forces of evil are always plotting and planning, ready to pounce. You must be brave and sensible and good. If you think of others before you think of yourself, you won't go far wrong. Now, that's enough chinwagging from me. Philip and I must be on our way. Goodbye everyone, and good luck!'

The castle rang with cheers as Philip and Mr Edgar walked across the courtyard and away over the drawbridge. Sergeant Robin dived down from one of the walls and flew ahead of them to the edge of the forest.He perched on a bush and sang a last little goodbye-song as they walked past him. Then he took off and flew back towards the turrets and towers of the castle. They watched him go, then they turned and headed along the forest path.

Autumn had coloured the trees and the sun shone down through a mass of red and yellow and golden leaves. Shafts of sunlight caught the jewelled dewdrops on spiders' webs in the bushes and the air was filled with the scent of ripe fruit and fresh nuts.

Philip felt fit and strong and the clear sharpness of the day made him want to run and skip along the path but he walked slowly so that Mr Edgar could keep up. The old beaver was always laughing at what he called his 'shaky pins' but he seemed slower and more unsteady than ever and Philip wondered if he was really fit enough to make a long journey.

Suddenly the old beaver grabbed hold of Philip's hand and pulled him back.

'Shh!' Mr Edgar said as Philip opened his mouth to speak.

The old beaver cocked his head to listen. Philip stayed silent and listened with him. He couldn't hear anything but Mr Edgar's sharp ears must have picked up some sound because he pulled Philip behind a tree.

'What is it?' Philip whispered.

'We're being followed,' Mr Edgar said.

CHAPTER THREE

Philip crouched down behind the tree and pressed himself against the trunk, trying to make himself as small as possible. He held his breath and listened.

At first, the forest seemed silent but then he heard the sound of footsteps rustling through the fallen leaves. The sound got closer and closer. Philip felt Mr Edgar grow tense, then suddenly the old beaver leaped out on to the path. Philip scrambled to his feet and followed.

There was a squeak of surprise and Philip caught sight of two small creatures diving into the bushes at the side of the path.

'Baby B! Nick! Come out at once!' Mr Edgar barked.

The little beaver and the hedgehog shuffled out

on to the path and stood looking down at the ground.

'What the drat are you two rascals up to?' Mr Edgar said. 'Are you following us?'

'Only a little bit,' Baby B mumbled, still not daring to look up.

'Well, turn round this instant and get yourselves back to Beaver Towers. Your mother and father will be worried out of their fur about you.'

'Oh, Grandpa, it's not fair,' Baby B cried. 'We want to come with you and Flipip, don't we, Nick?'

'Yes,' said the little hedgehog. 'We want to have adventures like you.'

Mr Edgar chuckled and bent down and tapped Nick gently on the snout.

'Well, you'll probably have plenty of adventures here at Beaver Towers,' he said. 'I'm relying on you two to keep the old place safe and sound from danger while I'm away.'

'Yes, but we looked on the list of jobs,' Baby B cut in, 'and we only got smelly things to do. Like, Nick's got to do polishing Doris the car. And I've got to do smelly washering-up. It's not fair – we're the ones who can do think-talking but . . .'

'Now, now! Don't you start getting swell-headed, you young whippersnapper. Think-talking is a gift. Use it for silly reasons or get too big for your boots and the gift will fly off and leave you. Always remember the old rhyme:

You must earn it to learn it.
Misuse it, and you'll lose it.

'Now then, no more chit-chat – you get off home at once. Quickly!'

Baby B and Nick turned and began to walk sadly along the path towards Beaver Towers. They stopped once and glanced back but Mr Edgar pointed his paw towards the castle and the two little animals went on their way again.

'Oh, dear me,' Mr Edgar sighed when they finally disappeared. 'I hope I'm doing the right thing, leaving them like this. Think-talking is such a powerful thing. It always attracts the notice of the powers of evil. And I've got a nasty feeling in my bones . . .'

'What about?' Philip asked.

'Oh, nothing certain – just a feeling that there's danger in the air.'

A moment before, the forest had been warm and bright but now there seemed to be dark shadows everywhere. They walked on without speaking and their eyes darted to every movement – each tremble of a leaf, each sway of a branch. They didn't see anyone but Philip couldn't stop feeling that they were being watched.

When they finally came out of the forest on to a broad, sunlit meadow, Philip let out a sigh of relief. Crowds of small, blue butterflies flickered round them as they walked and the warm sun drove away the last shivers of fear. Mr Edgar began humming a tune and Philip joined in.

They waded across a river, then passed some houses where rabbits were busy working in their gardens. The rabbits waved and wished them luck, then went on planting their carrots. Just beyond the houses, the path sloped away and they came to the sea.

There was a big hut on the beach and they opened it up and dragged one of the boats out on to the sand and down to the water's edge. Mr Edgar showed Philip how to raise the mast and hoist the sail, then they pushed the boat away from the shore and clambered on board.

A breeze filled the sail and they skimmed away across the waves. They followed the coast for a while then turned and headed out into the open sea.

As their little boat passed Round Rock Island a pair of red, serpent eyes watched them from inside the shadows of the cave. The eyes stared and stared until the boat grew tiny and finally disappeared over the horizon. The eyes closed in satisfaction. A moment later they snapped open again.

'Retsnom!' the Prince of Darkness' voice rumbled into the depths of the echoey cave. 'Retsnom! Come! The time for your work is almost here.'

A huge, black, glistening lump oozed and

slithered its way from the darkness, leaving a trail of slime on the cave floor.

'First,' said the Prince of Darkness, patting the wet, flabby skin of the creature, 'you must change your shape so that the fools will find you attractive. A bird, perhaps.'

The Prince of Darkness stood back as the creature transformed itself into the shape of a large raven. The blackness of its feathers and the glisten of its dark eyes were the only reminders of what it had been.

'Yes,' said the Prince of Darkness, 'but still not attractive enough. The fools like creatures they can pity, so let's give them something they can feel sorry for.'

He took hold of the bird and with one cruel movement he snapped the bone that ran the length of its wing. The raven squawked with pain then hopped around, trailing its broken wing.

'Perfect,' laughed the Prince of Darkness. 'Now listen. I must leave because I have some fine, evil work to do elsewhere. Deliver Beaver Towers to me when I return and I shall reward you well. Take your time. Let them work their own downfall. Wait for them to come to you, for come they surely will. Then strike! Fill them with fear and confusion! And they will be ours!'

CHAPTER FOUR

In the school room at Beaver Towers, the young animals were learning the names of plants.

Everybody was working hard except for Baby B and Nick. They were so busy whispering to each other that they didn't see their teacher, Mr Stripe, come up behind them. He banged his paw on their desk and they both jumped with shock.

'Baby B and Nick!' thundered the old badger. 'You two are impossible this week. Baby B, go and sit next to Rufus Rabbit.'

'But Rufus is in the hinfants. And he's always asking silly questions. It's not fair,' Baby B grumbled as he made his way up to the front of the class and sat down next to the little rabbit.

'When you stop behaving like an infant, you can go back and sit with the bigger animals,' Mr Stripe said sharply, and he looked so fierce that Baby B didn't dare say anything else.

It didn't stop him complaining to Mrs Badger, though, when he dropped in to see her after school.

'Well, my dear,' she said when he finished telling her, 'Mr Stripe was quite right – you were behaving like an infant. And I've heard from some of the animals in the kitchen that you haven't been doing the washing-up properly either.'

'Yes, but it's not fair. I must have to do everything – smelly school and smelly washering-up and then I must have to do think-talking because there's only me and Nick what's clever enough to do it.'

'Baby B!' Mrs Badger said, putting her knitting down and peering at him. 'I hope you're not becoming the kind of animal who boasts and doesn't pull their weight when it comes to work.'

The little beaver's face turned red and he shook his head.

'Good,' Mrs Badger said, then went back to her knitting.

Baby B stood awkwardly for a few minutes, not saying anything. He was just about to say goodbye and go when he noticed a freshly-baked cake in the middle of the table. He felt rather hungry and he always loved Mrs Badger's cakes. He knew she had probably baked it for a special occasion but he wished she would offer him a slice right now.

Mrs Badger looked up and asked, 'Would you like a slice of cake, Baby B?'

He was so surprised that it took him a moment before he said, 'Yes, please.'

Mrs Badger cut a big slice for him. It was delicious and when he finished it he found himself wishing he could have another, bigger, bit.

As soon as he thought it, Mrs Badger said, 'Would you like another slice, Baby B? A bigger one, perhaps?'

Baby B was so amazed that he forgot he was hungry and said, 'No thank you, I'm all fulled up.'

Then he had a hard job not to giggle with excitement. It was almost as if he had made Mrs Badger do something, just by thinking about it.

At seven o'clock that evening Baby B and Nick met in the library at Beaver Towers. There was something magical about the room with its rows and rows of lovely old books and it was the best place to concentrate for think-talking.

They sat on the floor next to Mr Edgar's leather chair and held paws. They closed their eyes and started to think. Where was Mr Edgar? Somewhere far away.

For a moment nothing happened, then suddenly they both jolted upright and gripped each other's paw tighter. They were still in the library but they could see Mr Edgar sitting in the little boat, and it felt just as if they were there with him. They could hear the slap of the waves against the boat and they could smell the salt of the sea.

'Hello, you two rascals,' Mr Edgar said, smiling and dropping the anchor over the side of the boat. 'Philip has just swum ashore and I'm going to wait for him here.'

'What's Flipip doing, Grandpa?'

'He's going to visit an old friend of mine called Master Omar. He's a great teacher and he lives in that lighthouse.'

Baby B and Nick turned their heads and they could see the tall, rocky island that rose out of the sea like a mountain. Way, way up at the top was a lighthouse, flashing its warning across miles and miles of ocean. Down at the bottom of the cliffs they could see Philip wade out of the water and start to climb the steps that snaked all the way up to the lighthouse.

'Now then, what have you got to report about Beaver Towers?' Mr Edgar asked.

'Oh, nothing,' Baby B sighed. 'No adventures nor nothing!'

'So,' chuckled Mr Edgar, 'you're miserable because everyone is safe and well, is that it?'

'No, but it's a bit very boring *and* I must have to sit with the hinfants as well,' Baby B groaned.

'Now, now, young 'un,' Mr Edgar said. 'Remember our motto – "Always Eager. Always Busy". No time to be bored, you know. Got to keep your eyes peeled and your ears pricked for the first sign of danger. If not, you might have more adventure than you bargained for. And above all, don't use your powers for anything silly. Now off you pop, and report back to me next week.'

Baby B and Nick took one last look at Mr Edgar in the rocking boat, then they closed their eyes and let go of each other's paw.

When they opened their eyes again, they were back in the library.

'Farewell and take care, you young scamps,' Mr Edgar said as soon as he felt the think-talking stop.

Then he looked up at the rocky island.

'And you, young Philip, you must take care as well. Master Omar's lessons can sometimes prove to be very dangerous indeed.'

CHAPTER FIVE

Philip reached the top of the steps and stood for a moment to get his breath back. From up here he could see the last bit of the sun dipping below the horizon as if its fire was being put out by the sea. The light from the lighthouse flashed out into the growing darkness.

Behind him, the door in the lighthouse opened and Master Omar's voice called, 'Come in.'

By the time he got inside and started to climb the spiral staircase, all Philip could see of Master Omar were his wellington boots on the stairs above. Finally, they reached the top level – a round room where the light slowly revolved, sending its beam out through the glass walls.

Master Omar stood in the shadows near the door and Philip couldn't see his face.

'Don't look at me,' Master Omar said. 'Stand beneath the light and turn with it. Just watch the light as it shines its message out into the world. Only the light.'

There was nothing fierce or strict about the voice but Philip knew he had to obey. He started to turn with the light, keeping his eyes fixed on the beam as it swept across the dark ocean.

He counted three turns then the whole room began to spin. There was a roaring in his ears, then silence. A silence that gradually gave way to a bubbling sound.

His body felt cool and soft. A gentle, rippling wave started at his feet and moved up through his body, sending it swaying backwards and forwards. He opened his eyes. He was in water. Deep, salty sea water that rocked him to and fro. He felt his arm floating upwards. He glanced at it and saw, not an arm, but a tiny strand of seaweed. He looked down and his whole body was a small, green plant.

He should have been afraid, but he wasn't. He felt very calm.

Time passed. A long, long time.

A shrimp came bobbing towards him. Its legs reached out and clasped on to him. The shrimp's mouth opened. Again he should have been afraid but he wasn't. The mouth closed over him. There was a tearing sound, then a little wrench as he was pulled from the rock. Then nothing.

Time passed.

He found himself bobbing through the water, nosing into clumps of weed. There were other creatures feeding too. Shrimps – like him. He clasped on to a plant. A plant such as he had been. He bit into its greenness. It tasted good.

Time passed.

A large fish came swimming out of the green darkness, lazily flapping the edges of its wide, flat body. It glided among the weeds with its mouth open, sucking in water and shrimps. Philip felt a stirring of fear as the fish turned to him. He felt the water begin to pull him and, with a rush and a tumble, he was sucked into that white mouth.

Time passed.

He felt his arms and shoulders rippling up and down and he saw below him the sandy bottom of the sea. He was moving lazily through the water, his eyes searching for shrimps.

He was a fish.

He found a group of shrimps and flapped over them, sucking them into his mouth. They tasted good.

Time passed.

There were other fish. Hundreds of them. All like him. He was swimming with them, turning and gliding with them, diving and soaring with them. They moved as if they were one.

Suddenly, above them, they saw a huge, dark shape and they scattered in all directions.

And now Philip was afraid. The shape was

diving towards him. It was a shark and he knew it had chosen him. Its teeth opened to show the rows of teeth. He twisted and turned to try to get away but there was a sharp stabbing pain as the teeth bit through him. Then there was nothing.

Time passed.

Philip could feel his muscles whipping his tail from side to side. He could feel the power and smoothness of his glide as he cruised through the water.

Beneath him, a shadow moved across the sea floor. A large, menacing shadow. His shadow. He was a shark.

He saw a shoal of fish below; fish with lazy, flapping wings. Fish such as he had been.

He plunged, his eyes fixed on just one of the fish. The shoal scattered in all directions but he kept his eyes on that one fish. His jaws opened. The fish tried to twist and turn away but he was too fast. His jaws closed and he felt his teeth sink into flesh, felt the snap of bone. Blood ran in his mouth. It tasted good.

Time passed.

A voice said, 'And so on, and so on. Round and round like the light. Look at the light.'

Philip opened his eyes.

He was in the lighthouse. Above him the light was still turning, flashing out across the water. In the shadows near the door stood Master Omar.

'Well, did you understand?' Master Omar asked.

'I think so. It's all linked, like a chain.'

Master Omar nodded.

'It's funny,' Philip went on, remembering how good it felt to eat the fish. 'When I was the fish I felt one thing, and when I was the shark I felt something else.'

'Point of view,' Master Omar said.

'It's complicated.'

'The truth is always complicated,' Master Omar said and then raised his hand as Philip opened his mouth to speak again. 'It is time for you to go. I must tend the light.'

Philip went to the top of the stairs and then looked back. Master Omar had his back to him, already working at the lonely, important job of keeping the light burning and turning.

'Thank you,' Philip said.

Master Omar nodded.

Philip started the long climb back down to the waiting boat.

CHAPTER SIX

Mr Edgar's old car, Doris, stood in the centre of the courtyard at Beaver Towers. Every centimetre of the car already sparkled but that didn't stop the two hedgehogs, Ann and Mick, from polishing her. As they rubbed away at the chrome and the paintwork with their dusters, they began singing their song:

> *Rub, rub, polish, shine*
> *Lovely little car of mine.*
> *Rub, rub, till you gleam.*
> *We are your loyal cleaning team.*

'Ha! Loyal cleaning team, indeed!' Mick said when they got to the end of the song. 'Not now that Nick has got so big-headed, we're not.'

At this very moment, Baby B and Nick came out of the castle door and started jumping down the steps. Ann spotted them and scuttled across the courtyard, followed by Mick.

'Nicholas Hedgehog!' Ann said in her fiercest voice. 'You're late. We started work on Doris ten minutes ago.'

'Well ... erm ... you see ... erm ...' Nick stammered.

'Yes?' Ann demanded.

'Well,' Nick went on when Baby B gave him a nudge, 'I don't think I should have to ... to do work because ... because me and Baby B do think-talking.'

'Stuff and nonsense!' shouted Mick. 'We're the Mechanics. We look after Doris. We are her loyal cleaning team. You can't just suddenly stop. We need you for the Nic bit at the end. Without you, we're the Mechans – and that just sounds silly. Besides, you used to love Doris.'

'I do still love her,' Nick said, giving a quick glance to where the car stood with sunlight sparkling on her body, 'but ...'

'But what?' Ann said, pushing her snout right up against his. 'Too lazy now, are you? See if we care. We don't need you. I'm strong enough to do your work in half the time because you're just a weak baby anyway!'

With that, she grabbed Mick's paw and pulled him away across the courtyard to Doris.

'I'm not a weak baby!' Nick shouted, but they didn't even look at him. They got out their dusters and began polishing Doris.

Nick watched them for a moment and his eyes grew bright with longing.

'I do miss Doris,' he said sadly. 'And I bet she misses me because I was best at polishing her headlights and her door handles. I wonder . . .'

And he was off – running across the courtyard until he got to the car. He grabbed a duster from the ground and began polishing at once. Mick and Ann started singing their song and Nick joined in.

They all looked so happy, working away together, that Baby B decided to go and have a look in the kitchen. He almost turned back when he saw the big pile of dirty plates, but once the sink was full of soapy water he began to enjoy himself.

Soon he was busy blowing colourful bubbles round the kitchen and there was a big puddle of water on the floor from all his splashing. It took him a very long time to finish washing the plates but it has to be said that in the end they sparkled nearly as much as Doris did.

The next day at school, Baby B asked if he could go back to his place next to Nick but Mr Stripe said he still had to sit with the infants. The little beaver slumped down next to Rufus Rabbit. And he was so sulky during the lesson on Tracks that he didn't put his paw up once, even when he knew the answer to the questions.

Then, just as Mr Stripe started the next lesson on berries, Baby B suddenly remembered what had happened with Mrs Badger and the cake. He concentrated very hard and pushed his thoughts out towards Mr Stripe.

Almost at once, the old teacher turned round from the blackboard where he was drawing a honeysuckle berry and said, 'Baby B, you can go back and sit in your proper place now.'

Baby B jumped up with a big grin on his face and ran back to his old seat.

'That was lucky,' Nick whispered.

'It wasn't lucky – it was me,' Baby B whispered as he sat down next to his friend. 'Watch.'

Again Baby B concentrated very hard.

Suddenly Mr Stripe yawned, sat down at his desk, and fell fast asleep.

For almost a minute nobody dared to move, then one of the older lambs tiptoed to the front and nudged Mr Stripe's shoulder. The old badger started to snore very loudly and the whole class giggled.

Soon they were all running around, shouting and laughing and throwing bits of paper at each other. A couple of the cheekier fieldmice got up on to Mr Stripe's desk and took turns to jump over the tip of his snout. Then a squirrel even climbed on to Mr Stripe's head and began to imitate his deep, growly voice. Everybody rolled around the floor laughing helplessly.

The only one not laughing was Nick.

'It's not funny, Baby B,' the little hedgehog said. 'Poor Mr Stripe.'

His voice was so sad that Baby B stopped giggling. He looked at Mr Stripe and suddenly saw what Nick meant. The two fieldmice had got hold of the badger's ears and were wiggling them backwards and forwards to make the squirrel laugh. Meanwhile, all the lambs were marching round the desk making silly snoring noises.

Baby B felt so sorry for what he'd done that he immediately shouted, 'Watch out! Mr Stripe's going to wake up.'

While the animals were all dashing back to their desks, Baby B sent his thoughts out to Mr Stripe.

The old teacher stirred and stood up.

'Now, where was I?' he said as if he'd simply forgotten what he was doing. 'Oh yes, the honey-suckle berry. So, who can tell me the difference between that berry and the whortleberry?'

The rest of the lesson went on as if nothing had happened, and Baby B made his mind up never to try to make Mr Stripe look silly again.

A week later, though, Mr Stripe made an announcement.

'Now,' he growled, 'during this weekend I want you to find something to bring to school on Monday for Show and Tell.'

'Something from home, Mr Stripe?' asked Rufus Rabbit.

'Yes, or from anywhere on the island.'

At once, Baby B had an idea and, almost without realizing what he was doing, he sent his thoughts to Mr Stripe.

The teacher blinked and then started repeating what Baby B was thinking.

'In fact,' Mr Stripe said, 'I would like some of you to go somewhere else. To . . . to Round Rock Island, perhaps. Yes, that's a good idea. Two of you can go over there and bring back something really interesting for Show and Tell. Now, who shall I choose? Baby B and Nick.'

Baby B noticed how difficult it was to think-talk to Mr Edgar that evening. Mr Edgar said he could hardly hear what they were saying but Baby B didn't care.

At last he was going to have an adventure.

CHAPTER SEVEN

'I can't imagine what Mr Stripe was thinking about, sending you off to Round Rock Island like this,' Mrs Badger grumbled as she packed some sandwiches into a small picnic basket.

'It's for Toe and Shell,' Baby B said.

'Show and Tell, dear,' Mrs Badger corrected.

'That's right. And it's millions exciting because it's an adventure, isn't it, Nick?'

The little hedgehog nodded but he didn't look entirely sure that he wanted this kind of adventure.

'That's all well and good,' Mrs Badger went on, putting a couple of large slices of cake into the basket, 'but I don't like the idea of the two of you going off on your own.'

'We're not hinfants, Mrs Badger. We're growed up and riskonstable like Mr Edgar said.'

'Hmm, well, I just hope you are,' Mrs Badger said, handing Baby B the picnic basket. 'Now, don't go eating this until lunchtime. And be back here by five o'clock, otherwise I'll be on the warpath – and that's not a pretty sight, I can tell you!'

Five minutes after they left the castle, Baby B felt hungry so they started eating the sandwiches. By the time they got to the beach there were only the two slices of cake left. Nick said it would be silly to take a nearly-empty picnic basket with them so they ate the cake too.

'We can do fishing for lunch. I'm good at swimming and catching fish,' Baby B said as they pulled the small boat out of the hut and into the sea.

'I'm not very good at swimming and catching fish,' Nick gulped as he sat in the boat and it began to rock up and down with the waves. 'Because I don't really love the sea – it's a bit too wet for me.'

'That's all right, I can do the sailoring,' Baby B said. 'You sit there and close your eyes.'

In fact, Nick did more than close his eyes – he closed his eyes, hid under the seat, and rolled himself up into a ball.

It was probably just as well because he might have been very scared if he'd seen Baby B trying to sail the boat. First of all, the little beaver got his paw tangled up in one of the ropes while he was raising the sail and he ended up hanging upside down from the mast. Then, when he bit through the rope with his sharp teeth, he fell down and the sail fell on top of him.

It took him ages to scramble out from under the sail and even longer to get it raised again because now the rope was too short to tie properly. So he had to hold on to the rope with one paw and try to steer the boat with the other. This meant that sometimes the sail slipped down because he wasn't pulling hard enough on the rope, and sometimes the boat went round and round in circles because he couldn't keep the tiller straight.

Luckily the sea wasn't very rough and the wind was blowing in the right direction. An hour later the boat slid on to the beach of Round Rock Island.

'You are clever, Baby B,' Nick said when he unrolled himself and saw where they were.

'Oh, I'm just a good sailorer,' Baby B said proudly. Then he let go of the rope and the sail fell down on top of his head again.

After all that, Round Rock Island turned out to be a disappointment. They went from one side of it to the other, but there was nothing to see except bare rock. It was good fun to stand on top of the cliff and throw stones down into the sea. And Baby B had an adventure when he got too close to the edge and almost fell over, but Nick grabbed the straps of his dungarees just in time.

They threw stones for nearly an hour but then

they started to get hungry so they went down to the beach again. Baby B dashed into the sea to catch some fish for lunch but every time he dived, he came back up with empty paws.

'I've got some seaweed,' he said as he finally came ashore. 'Seaweed is millions good to eat for hedgehogs, it makes their spikes go all sharp.'

Nick took a little nibble but he said it was a bit too salty and anyway his spikes were sharp enough and he thought it was time to go home for a proper lunch.

'We can't go home now,' Baby B said. 'We haven't had adventures and we haven't even found things for Toe and Shell.'

Just at that moment he saw something move in the entrance to a cave halfway up the cliff.

'Look!' he shouted. 'There's something in that cave. It might be a pirate or something. Come on!'

Baby B raced away up the path towards the cave. Nick didn't really want to meet a pirate but he didn't want to be left alone on the beach either, so he scampered after his friend.

'It looks a bit dark in there,' Nick said when they got to the cave.

'I'm not scared,' Baby B said, but he took hold of Nick's paw before they started to tiptoe inside.

The deeper they ventured into the cave, the darker it grew. There was a tick-tock dripping sound that echoed in the darkness and the two friends gripped each other's paw tightly.

'It's a bit millions creepy-crawly in here,' Baby B whispered.

'P'raps we can go home for lunch,' Nick whispered back.

'P'raps we can,' Baby B agreed.

They both turned, then jumped into the air in fright.

A dark shape stood between them and the mouth of the cave. It hopped and flapped towards them and they both squealed and clung on to each other. Then suddenly it sank to the floor and lay still.

'It's only a bird,' Baby B said as his eyes got used to the dark.

'Yes, but it's a very big bird,' Nick said, tugging at Baby B's paw to stop him moving forward.

The bird tried to lift its broken wing then let it fall back to the floor. It hung its head and closed its eyes as if the pain was terrible.

'Oh, poor thing,' Baby B said gently. 'It's hurted itself.'

The bird half opened one of its eyes and peeped out slyly, then it made a soft sobbing sound.

'Oh listen, it's crying,' Baby B said, tears springing to his own eyes. 'We must have to help it. We can take it back home and make it all better. Mrs Badger can look after it.'

'Baby B, I don't think it's a good idea,' Nick began, but the little beaver cut him off.

'Come on, Nick. We must help it. And it can be

our Toe and Shell for Mr Stripe. It will be the bestest Toe and Shell of anyone. Come on!'

Step by step they helped the bird limp down the path, across the beach, and into the boat. Then they set sail.

And that was how Retsnom came to Beaver Towers.

CHAPTER EIGHT

Mrs Badger said that Retsnom was too poorly to go to the schoolroom, so Mr Stripe's class came to her house for Baby B and Nick's Show and Tell. While the class looked at Retsnom, Mrs Badger took Mr Stripe into the kitchen and made him a cup of tea.

'You've made an excellent job of that splint on the bird's wing, ma'am,' Mr Stripe said. 'He should be well in no time. Did he say how he came to be injured?'

Mrs Badger shook her head. 'He told me his name and that's all. Sergeant Robin came to talk to him but he wouldn't speak to him either. In fact, Sergeant Robin was rather frightened by him, and I must confess that I am too. He gave me a couple of nasty pecks while I was trying to mend his wing.'

'Well, we can't just send him away while he's still injured,' Mr Stripe said.

'No, of course not – I wouldn't dream of it,' Mrs Badger agreed, 'but I think we must keep a close eye on him. I have a funny feeling in my bones that he could be a danger to us all.'

It took two weeks before Retsnom's wing was strong enough to have the splint taken off. During that time, Baby B and Nick went to see him every day. They weren't sure why they went because they were both rather scared of him, but it was as if something made them go. Every day after school they stood looking at Retsnom while he stared at them with his glittering eyes. Not a word was spoken.

One night, Baby B woke up shouting and screaming – he had been having a horrible nightmare. He couldn't remember much about it except that there had been a dark cave and a horrible, slimy monster.

When he told Nick about it the next day, the little hedgehog's mouth fell open in surprise.

'Oh, Baby B,' he said, 'I don't like it. I had that dream too.'

They both shivered.

Another thing that worried them was that it was getting harder and harder to think-talk. Baby B knew that it was because he was using his powers to do silly things, like making Mr Stripe forget to give them homework, but he couldn't help it – a voice inside him kept telling him to do it.

Most evenings Baby B and Nick still managed to get a fuzzy think-talking picture in their heads and they were able to tell Mr Edgar and Philip what was going on at Beaver Towers, but they never mentioned Retsnom. Then, for two days, they couldn't get any picture at all.

Baby B was really worried and the next day he made an extra-special effort to be good. He went round to Mrs Badger's after school and helped her clean her house because she was feeling very tired. He broke one of the plates he was washing up and he left a trail of muddy paw prints on the floor when he was mopping up the water he had spilt, but Mrs Badger said it was a very kind thought anyway.

That evening, when he and Nick sat together in the library, they concentrated very hard and they suddenly got a clear picture in their heads.

'Oh, there you are at last,' Mr Edgar said clearly and loudly. 'I was beginning to get a bit worried about you. What have you been up to?'

They told Mr Edgar what had happened at the castle since they had last spoken to him, then they looked around to see where he was this time.

He was standing at the edge of a desert. Philip was next to him, with a big smile on his face.

'Flipip!' Baby B shouted with joy.

'Hello, Baby B. Hello, Nick,' Philip said. 'It's

great to see you. I hope you're not getting into too much mischief!'

'No,' Baby B said but he felt a guilty blush in his cheeks and the think-talking picture became a bit fainter. 'Are you having millions of adventures, Flipip?'

'Not adventures exactly,' Philip said. 'But it's very interesting and I'm learning lots of things.'

'Like going to school?' Nick asked.

'A bit,' Philip laughed. 'I'm just going to meet someone for my next lesson. In there.'

Baby B and Nick looked to where Philip was pointing and they saw a walled city stretching away up a hillside. The houses all had flat roofs and were huddled together around a maze of narrow alleyways. Some camels and donkeys were standing next to a palm tree just outside the gate to the city.

Philip patted one of the donkeys as he walked past, then he turned and waved to Baby B and Nick before he went through the gate and into the city.

CHAPTER NINE

The alleyways of the city were crowded with people dressed in robes and all the women had veils across their faces. A rich smell filled the air from the stalls of fruit and vegetables and herbs and spices that were set up along the walls.

As Philip made his way through the jostling crowds he glanced into doorways and saw workshops, with goldsmiths and silversmiths and carpet weavers and dyers and carpenters, all hard at work at their crafts.

He came to a small square with eight alleyways branching out in different directions. Now, which one had Mr Edgar told him to take? Oh yes, the third one on the right next to the little fountain set in the wall. Now, the fourth doorway along this alleyway . . .

Philip pushed open the door and walked into a large courtyard where the bright sunlight made him blink after the darkness of the alleyways. A lemon tree stood in the centre of the courtyard and from one of the branches hung a cage. Inside the cage, a canary, the same colour as the ripe lemons, was singing a beautiful melody.

Philip crossed the courtyard and knocked on the lightblue door of the house.

'Come in,' said a woman's voice.

Philip opened the door and stepped inside.

He just had time to notice the bare white walls and the polished wooden floors, then he closed the door behind him and the room was very dark. The only light came from a small, flickering candle inside a red glass jar that hung from the high ceiling.

'Sit,' said the woman's voice, and Philip sat down on the floor.

All he could see of the woman was a dark shape in the corner of the room. Her voice sounded young but there was something about the shape that made him feel she was very old.

'Who are you?' she asked.

'Philip.'

'Yes, but *who* are you?'

'I'm sorry, I don't understand,' Philip said, wondering if perhaps he had come to the wrong house.

'Which part of you is Philip?'

'All of me.'

'I see. So, your body is you, is it?'

'Yes, I think so,' Philip said, feeling that perhaps this wasn't the right answer.

'And if I cut off one of your hands, would you still be you?'

'Yes,' Philip whispered, suddenly afraid that she might do what she said.

'So you are not your hand then?'

'No.'

'And if I cut off your arms and your legs, would you still be you? And if I took out your eyes and cut off your ears and your tongue so that you couldn't see or hear or talk, would you still be you?'

'I think so,' Philip said with a shiver at the thought of all those things being done to him. Then he had a sudden thought. 'Perhaps I am my brain.'

'Perhaps,' the woman said, 'but perhaps not. For example, you have a dog called Megs, don't you?'

'Yes!' Philip gasped, amazed that she knew about Megs.

'Well, I want you to think about her for a moment. Try to see her clearly in your mind.'

Philip thought, and he could see Megs curled up in front of the fire at home. He saw the way her head rested on her paws and how her tail curled across her back legs.

'Good,' said the woman. 'Now tell your brain to stop thinking about her.'

Philip tried. But the more he tried, the more he kept thinking about her. Even when he managed to stop the picture, his brain kept whispering the name 'Megs' over and over.

'So?' asked the woman.

'Well, I wanted to stop thinking but my brain wouldn't listen to me. And it was like I just had to watch what my brain wanted to do.'

'Exactly – you were watching your brain.'

'So, who am I then?' Philip asked.

'The watcher, perhaps.'

'But . . .' Philip began.

'I know no more than that,' the woman said. Then she laughed gently and added, 'Sometimes I don't even know that. Now you must go back to Mr Edgar. But never forget that you are perhaps not what you seem to be.'

Philip stood up and walked to the door. He opened it and the bright sunlight almost blinded him. He turned back and looked at the corner of the room where the woman had been.

She had gone. There was just the stool where she had been sitting.

Philip crossed the courtyard where the canary was still singing and he went out into the noisy bustle of the city.

CHAPTER TEN

Retsnom disappeared.

Baby B and all the other pupils were sitting in the classroom doing a test on plants when the door burst open and Mrs Badger rushed in.

'Oh, Mr Stripe,' she panted. 'Something's happened.'

'What is it, Mrs Badger? Do sit down, you look all hot and bothered,' Mr Stripe said, offering her his chair.

'I am, oh, I am,' she said, sitting down and starting to fan her face with her apron. 'I've been running all over the place, searching high and low, but he's gone.'

'Who's gone, my dear?'

'Retsnom, Mr Stripe. I left him in the sitting room while I went into the kitchen to bake a chocolate cake and when I went back, he was gone. I searched all over the house, then I spotted this next to an open window.'

She felt in her apron pocket and pulled out a black feather.

'Hmm, this definitely comes from a raven's tail,' Mr Stripe said, holding the feather up and peering at it. 'But it has a rather strange feel to it – almost slimy.'

'That's why I'm sure it's Retsnom's feather,' Mrs Badger said. 'His whole body had a nasty slimy feel – I could hardly bear to touch him while I was putting the splint on his wing.'

'Do all ravens' feathers feel slimy, Mr Stripe?' asked Rufus Rabbit.

'Oh, don't be such a hinfant, Rufus,' Baby B scoffed. 'Mr Stripe said it was strange, didn't he?'

'Baby B, don't be unkind to an animal younger than yourself,' Mr Stripe said.

'But he's always askering silly questions just so you think he's working hardest and he . . .' Baby B stopped when he saw the fierce look his teacher was giving him.

'Well, ma'am,' Mr Stripe said, turning back to Mrs Badger, 'I'd say that if Retsnom has gone, we're all better off without him.'

'Oh, I shan't miss him, I'll grant you that,' Mrs Badger replied. 'But now we don't know where he is or what kind of mischief he's up to. And mark my words, he's up to something wicked – I can feel it in my bones.'

For the next two days, all the animals joined in a search of the island without finding a single clue. Then Sergeant Robin came flying back with the news that he'd spotted some raven's feathers underneath an oak tree in the middle of the forest.

Everybody dashed to the tree and what they saw made them all shiver.

There was no sign of Retsnom but the tree was starting to wither. The leaves had turned black, the bark was peeling, and a thick, green slime was oozing from the trunk.

Mr Stripe picked up the feathers and looked at them.

'Yes, they belong to Retsnom all right,' he said. 'He must have perched in this tree.'

'But why has the tree all gone horrible?' Nick asked.

'I don't know,' Mr Stripe murmured. 'I just don't know. I've never seen anything like it.'

During the next week, though, Mr Stripe and all the others saw plenty of things like it. All over the forest hundreds of trees started to wither exactly like the oak tree.

'It's so terrible, Mr Stripe,' Mrs Badger said as they walked round the courtyard of Beaver Towers one day. 'Whatever are we going to do?'

'I think the time has come to get some advice

from Mr Edgar,' Mr Stripe replied. 'We'll get Baby B and Nick to ask for help.'

But Baby B and Nick couldn't contact Mr Edgar.

They sat in the library every evening and concentrated as hard as they could, but nothing happened. Baby B kept saying that perhaps it was because Mr Edgar and Philip were too far away, but he couldn't help remembering the rhyme about think-talking:

> You must earn it to learn it.
> Misuse it, and you'll lose it.

Baby B was scared. Trees were dying all over the island. The rabbits said their carrots weren't growing. The sheep reported that the grass had started to shrivel and turn brown. Everybody noticed that the water in the wells looked cloudy and tasted strange. And Baby B's mother and father came back from fishing one day and announced that all the fish had disappeared from the rivers.

There was danger at Beaver Towers and they needed help, but they couldn't get it.

Then the dreams started.

CHAPTER ELEVEN

Retsnom was coming closer.

Baby B couldn't see him but he knew he was there, somewhere in the dark cave, and he could hear a slithering sound getting closer. He wanted to run away but when he tried to move his legs, they seemed stuck to the ground.

And now Retsnom was even closer – just round the corner of the cave. The slithering noise was getting louder and louder. Baby B opened his mouth to scream for help, but no sound came out.

Then, suddenly, he wasn't in the cave. He was floating through the forest, just below the tops of the trees. The sun was shining. A voice was calling to him.

'This way!' the voice called. 'This way! Come and see me. I am your friend.'

The voice was so gentle and kind that all the fears about the dark cave melted away. Baby B was excited and filled with longing. Soon he would see this new friend with the lovely voice. He would never be scared again because this friend would protect him and look after him.

He was floating across a big clearing in the forest now. He looked around and saw that all of the animals of the island were floating with him. And they all looked happy. They were smiling because they were going to see the friend with the lovely voice. The sun was shining down on them all.

'Here I am,' called the voice. 'Come to me. You'll be safe with me.'

And then they all saw him, standing at the top of a tree on the edge of the clearing.

It was Retsnom.

His wings were spread wide and the sun was shining on him so that all the colours of the rainbow seemed to glisten on his glossy feathers. He looked magnificent – so beautiful and powerful that the animals hardly dared to look at him.

Then Baby B woke up.

He lay awake in his bed until the morning, unable to go back to sleep.

Baby B was sitting in the classroom waiting for school to begin, when Nick came through the door and rushed straight over to him.

'I had another dream,' the little hedgehog

whispered. 'It was horrible. I was in this cave and there was this scary noise. And then I was flying in the forest and it was all lovely and then I saw Retsnom. Only he wasn't black and slimy, he was –'

'All the colours of the rainbow!' Baby B gasped. 'Oh Nick, we had the same dream.'

At that moment, Mr Stripe came into the room so they couldn't go on talking. But Baby B couldn't concentrate on the lesson. He kept thinking about the dream and, on top of that, he felt very tired because he had been awake so long during the night.

Then Baby B noticed that all the young animals were yawning. Everybody was tired – so tired, in fact, that one of the young squirrels and a couple of the badgers actually fell asleep at their desks and Mr Stripe had to wake them up.

'Wakey, wakey, you dozy creatures!' Mr Stripe growled as he shook their shoulders. Then he put his paw in front of his mouth and yawned himself. 'Oh dear, it must be catching! No, I know why I'm tired – I had a most peculiar dream last night and then I simply couldn't get back to sleep.'

Baby B and Nick's eyes were nearly popping out of their heads as they turned and looked at each other.

Mrs Badger was sleeping in her chair when Baby B and Nick arrived at her house after school.

She woke up with a start and then rubbed her eyes.

'Bless my soul, I must have been having forty winks! It's probably because I didn't sleep very well last night. I had a dream and then I couldn't get back to sleep.'

'We did have it as well!' Nick squeaked.

'Everybody did, even Rufus Rabbit,' Baby B added. 'It was about Retsnom.'

'That's right,' Mrs Badger said. 'Such a nice dream it was. I think we've all been most unfair to that poor creature – he's really very friendly and he just wants to help us.'

'No, Mrs Badger,' Baby B burst out. 'Me and Nick, we were talking after school and we think he's doing a sort of think-talk to hippotrize us so that we like him. That's what we think, don't we, Nick?'

The little hedgehog nodded.

'Hypnotize us? Bless my soul, what a silly idea!' Mrs Badger said. 'Besides, you can't hypnotize someone and make them do what they don't want to do.'

'Yes, but this is special hippotrizing while you are asleep!' Baby B went on. 'He wants us to like him and he's pertending to be nice but look what he's doing to the trees.'

'He's deading them and making all that green stuff come out of them,' Nick said, shivering.

'Really, you two do talk the most nonsense I've ever heard. Killing trees. Trying to hypnotize us.

Whatever will you think of next! Retsnom is our friend.'

'But, Mrs Badger, you said he was up to something wicked. You said you could feel it in your bones!' Baby B pointed out.

'Well, I was wrong!' Mrs Badger snapped. 'And I don't want you to say another word against Retsnom – do you hear?'

Baby B and Nick were shocked. Her voice was angry and severe. She stared at them so fiercely that she didn't even look like the Mrs Badger they both loved so much.

'Not another word, do you hear?' she snapped again.

They gulped and nodded but as soon as she went out to the kitchen, Baby B pointed to the front door. They tiptoed over to it.

Baby B lifted the latch as quietly as he could, then they ran away down the path and out of the garden gate. Only when they reached the safety of some trees at the other side of the field did they stop to catch their breath.

'It's true!' Baby B panted. 'He's hippotrizing everybody to make them do what he wants. Mrs Badger's the first one who believes him but soon it will be everybody. Oh Nick, what are we going to do?'

CHAPTER TWELVE

As Baby B got into bed that evening, he asked his mother if she could leave the night light burning in his room because he didn't want to sleep in the dark.

'What on earth are you scared of?' his mother asked as she tucked him up in bed.

'I keep having horrible dreams about Retsnom,' Baby B said, hoping she would give him a cuddle and stay with him for a while.

'They're not horrible at all. We've all been having dreams like that and they're lovely. Retsnom is our friend and you should be grateful you can dream about him. I can't wait to have another one tonight. Now, off to sleep with you and no more silliness!'

She blew out the night light and went straight

out of the room without even looking back at him. Normally she always let him have a night light if he wanted it and she never left the room without tickling his ears and giving him a goodnight kiss.

He wanted to call her back and tell her she had forgotten, but he knew it would do no good. She had been taken over by Retsnom.

Baby B lay in his bed and wiped a tear from his eye.

Well, he wouldn't go to sleep. That way he wouldn't let Retsnom come creeping into his dreams and try to make him think he was a nice, friendly bird. He wasn't. He was horrible and evil and Baby B wished he'd never gone to Round Rock Island and found him.

He wished he hadn't done silly things with his think-talking powers too. If only he could still contact Mr Edgar and Flipip. They would know what to do. But now he had no one to help him. Mrs Badger and his own mother already believed Retsnom and soon everybody else would too.

Suddenly Baby B heard the door to his bedroom click open. He lay very still in the dark and listened. Someone padded softly over to his bed. He could hear breathing right next to him.

'Baby B, wake up!'

'Nick!' Baby B whispered in relief. 'What are you doing here?'

'I don't like it very much in my bed in the dark by myself. Can I come in with you?'

'Yes, all right,' Baby B said, grateful that he wouldn't be alone in the night. 'But be careful with your spikes because they are millions prickerly.'

They lay in bed with the pillow between them so that Nick's spikes wouldn't prickle Baby B every time one of them moved.

It made the dark much less scary to be able to talk to each other. And even when they weren't talking, it was comforting to know there was a friend nearby in case of danger.

For a long time they kept awake by nudging each other every five minutes. But as it got later and later, they got more and more tired until Nick forgot to nudge Baby B and Baby B forgot to nudge Nick and they both fell fast asleep.

They were floating through the forest together. They crossed the sunlit clearing and saw the rainbow-coloured Retsnom talking to all the animals of the island. Mrs Badger, Mr Stripe, Mick, Baby B's mother and father – everyone was there and they were all looking up at Retsnom with smiles on their faces.

'I am your friend,' Retsnom was saying as Baby B and Nick floated nearer. 'I have come to help you all. But there are two silly animals who are not your friends. They are telling lies about me and trying to trick you all. And there they are!'

Retsnom pointed his wing at Baby B and Nick and all the animals turned and stared at them.

'They are your enemies,' Retsnom squawked.

'You must capture them and bring them to me. Now!'

Baby B woke up as he felt something stab into him. Nick had rolled right over the pillow and was lying on top of him moaning, 'No! No! Help!'

'Nick, wake up!' Baby B shouted, pushing the hedgehog off him and jumping out of bed.

'What is it?' Nick asked, jerking awake.

'We've got to go before they catch us!' Baby B said, pulling on his dungarees and getting the straps done up right at the very first go.

'Why?' Nick said.

'You saw the dream, didn't you? Retsnom is telling everybody that you and me are the henemy.'

Just then, they heard the sound of voices from all over the castle. The animals were waking up and rushing out of their rooms to do what Retsnom had told them. Baby B and Nick listened for a moment and then dashed for the door.

They fled along the corridor and started down the stairs. Baby B jumped them two at a time and Nick tried to copy him, but the little hedgehog lost his footing and went head over heels. He quickly rolled himself into a ball and bounced faster and faster until he reached the bottom before Baby B.

'Come on!' Baby B said as Nick unrolled himself. 'We've got to get downstairs to the Great Hall and out of the door before anyone sees us.'

They scampered along the landing to the main stairs. They were just about to race down them when a couple of rabbits ran into the Great Hall. They were quickly followed by Mick and a group of other animals.

Baby B and Nick pressed themselves back into the shadows at the top of the stairs.

'Nick's room is empty!' they heard Mick shout. 'He must be in Baby B's room. Come on, let's get them!'

Baby B and Nick heard them running up the stairs and for a moment they were too scared to move. Then the little beaver glanced along the corridor and saw the library door. Of course – the secret passageway!

'Quick, follow me!' he whispered to Nick.

They darted along the corridor and dived into the library just as the animals reached the top of the stairs and charged off in the other direction.

There was no time to lose. They ran to the bookcase and pulled. The bookcase swung open like a door and they looked down the steep stone stairs that led to the secret tunnel.

It was dark down there and they didn't want to go, but there was no other way. They stepped on to the first step and closed the bookcase behind them. Then, holding on to each other's paw, they started the long journey down the stairs and along the tunnel.

'We're safe,' Nick said, when they finally came out through a bunch of ferns at the end of the tunnel.

The moon came out from behind some clouds and lit up all the trees of the forest with its silver light.

Baby B hoped that Nick was right, but he couldn't help thinking that somewhere, out there in the forest, Retsnom was perched in his tree.

CHAPTER THIRTEEN

Baby B and Nick crept along the forest path.

The moon shone through the trees, casting scary shadows on the ground. Every few seconds the two young animals froze, their ears pricked and their eyes wide open to check for danger.

Suddenly, a wind blew across the forest, rattling branches and making the leaves whisper and flap. Baby B and Nick peered anxiously up at the trees. Perhaps Retsnom was up there somewhere, ready to swoop down and grab them with his sharp raven's claws.

The wind passed and silence fell. Now it was so quiet that they felt as if the noise from every step they took was echoing round the forest, telling their enemy where they were.

Hardly daring to breathe, they tiptoed onwards

through the heart of the forest. They moved so slowly that it took ages and ages before they came out of the trees and stood on the edge of the open fields.

The moonlight was so bright that if Retsnom was flying above the island he would see them at once. They hid under a clump of ferns and waited and waited until finally some big clouds rolled across the sky and covered up the moon.

'Come on, Nick,' Baby B whispered. 'If we do millions fast running we can get to the Manor before the moon comes out again.'

'Why is we going there?'

'Because I know a millions good place for hiding. Quick!'

Under cover of the darkness they sped across the fields and through the orchards that led to the Manor. Just as they reached the front door, the moon came out from behind the clouds and flooded everywhere with its cold light. They pushed open the door and darted inside.

The rambling old house belonged to Mr Edgar but Baby B and his parents had lived there for a while until they had moved into Beaver Towers. Now Mr Edgar used it as a place to stay when he wanted a bit of peace and quiet. Since he'd been away, nobody had been there and it smelled dusty and unlived in.

Baby B led the way along the corridor, down some twisting stone steps, along another corridor, and down some even twistier steps. He opened a door into a small room and ran straight across to the huge fireplace. Carved into the stone on the back wall of the fireplace was the figure of a beaver. Baby B reached up and pressed the flat tail of the figure, and the stone swung open to reveal a doorway.

'Where does it go?' Nick asked, peering down the steps inside.

'It's the cellar where Grandpa Edgar keeps the logs,' Baby B said. 'Nobody will ever finding us here. Come on.'

It was very dark in the cellar but they lit a small oil lamp and made themselves comfortable on a pile of logs. Although Mr Edgar was a long way away, it was good to be in his house. They could imagine him sitting in his favourite chair in front of the fire and they could almost hear his voice telling them not to worry. It made them feel safe at last.

It was still night-time and they were very tired but they didn't dare go to sleep in case they dreamed about Retsnom. Baby B made up a little tune and started humming it to help them keep awake. Nick joined in for a while but then he suddenly stopped and Baby B saw that he had tears in his eyes.

'Why are you all crying?' he asked.

'It's Mick,' sniffed the little hedgehog as a tear ran down his cheek. 'He's been my friend for ever and ever and now he doesn't like me any more. And he says I am a henemy and it's not true because I'm not a henemy, I'm me.'

'Oh, don't be sad,' Baby B said. 'It's not the proper Mick. It's only a hippotrized Mick, and that's not the same. It's like my mummy and daddy and Mrs Badger and Mr Stripe – they all love us really. But when you are hippotrized you don't know what you are doing.'

Nick had stopped crying but Baby B could see that his friend was still sad so he reached over to give him a little pat.

'Ow!' Baby B squeaked as his paw touched Nick's sharp spines. 'Why are you always so prickerly?'

'Because I'm a hedgehog,' Nick said. 'And if you haven't got any prickles you can't be a hedgehog.'

The idea of a hedgehog without any prickles made Baby B giggle and soon Nick saw the joke and started to giggle too. The giggles turned to laughter and they laughed so long and so hard that they both felt cheered up and they started to hum Baby B's tune again.

Then Baby B began to make up words for the tune and very soon they had a whole song and they sang it together. Baby B sang the long lines and Nick sang the short lines.

This is how it went:

> *Nick is a hedgehog who's prickerly,*
> *It's true!*

He's covered all over so thickerly,
Like glue!
With spines that lift up very trickerly,
They do!
Don't tickle him to make him feel tickerly,
Or you
Will soon run away millions quickerly,
Toodle-oo!
With a poor paw that feels very sickerly,
Boo-hoo!

They sang the song for the rest of the night and most of the morning too. It made them feel happy and it helped stop them from nodding off to sleep. Then, around lunchtime, they both started to get hungry and the gnawing pain in their tummies meant that they couldn't have fallen asleep even if they had wanted to.

'I'm starving,' Nick groaned towards the end of the afternoon.

'So am I,' said Baby B. 'Let's go and see if Mr Edgar has left anything in his cupboard.'

They crept upstairs to the cupboard but it was bare. They went into every room hoping to find something to eat – perhaps some nuts or even a few crumbs from one of Mrs Badger's delicious chocolate cakes that Mr Edgar loved so much – but there was nothing.

Then Baby B peeped out of the window to make sure that nobody was coming to search for them.

He looked across the fields and noticed all the apples lying on the ground in the orchards.

'Oh Nick, look!' he called.

Nick pressed his nose to the window and licked his lips. 'Yum, yum! I love apples. Can we go out and get some?'

'It's a bit too very dangerous,' Baby B said, shaking his head, but the apples looked too crisp and crunchy to resist. 'I know – we can wait until it's night, then we can run out and pick up some apples and come back before anyone sees us.'

'Yes, good idea,' Nick agreed, his mouth watering at the thought.

They sat by the window watching the sun sink oh-so-very slowly down behind the trees. Their tummies rumbled and grumbled as they waited but, finally, the last bit of light faded from the sky.

They opened the front door. It was dark, dark night out there and they were both scared, but their hunger was stronger than their fear.

They took a deep breath and ran out into the darkness.

CHAPTER FOURTEEN

It was dark and dangerous out in the orchard and the plan was to dash back to the Manor as soon as possible. But when Baby B and Nick smelled the apples, they couldn't resist taking a little bite. And once they had taken that first bite, they couldn't resist taking another. And another and another.

They quickly gobbled their way through one whole apple each – stalk and pips and all. It was so delicious and juicy that they forgot about everything else and stayed there, munching and crunching their way through a second apple and then a third. It was only when they heard a faint drumming sound in the distance that they stopped eating and looked up.

The noise grew louder and louder and the earth started to shake. It was the pounding of hooves.

Some creatures were galloping towards the Manor and they were coming fast. Nearer and nearer. There wasn't even time to run back indoors and hide.

Nick gave a little squeak of fear and rolled up into a ball.

'No, Nick,' Baby B said quickly. 'You'll get all treaded on there. Quick, grab hold of my tail!'

Baby B felt Nick grab his tail, then he sprang on to the nearest tree and scrambled up the trunk. They had just reached the first branch when they saw six sheep burst round the side of the Manor and gallop towards them through the orchard.

Baby B and Nick hid among the leaves and watched as the sheep thundered under the tree.

'Hurry, hurry!' the first sheep called to the others. 'Everyone to the castle! Retsnom is waiting.'

'Retsnom! Retsnom!' the others bleated as they raced away through the orchard and across the fields towards the forest.

They waited a while to make sure the sheep had gone and then Baby B climbed back down the tree. As soon as they were on the ground Nick let go of his tail and started running towards the Manor.

'Wait! Come back!' Baby B called.

'Why? We must go and hide again,' Nick said.

'We can't hide for ever and ever. We must do something. You heard the sheep – everybody is going to Beaver Towers. We must go and find out why.'

'Oh no, Baby B, I don't want to!'

Nick started running back to the Manor again but when he saw Baby B walking towards the forest, he turned round and ran after him.

'I don't like this idea, Baby B,' Nick panted when he caught up with him at the edge of the forest.

'You don't have to come if you don't want to,' Baby B said and he kept walking down the path into the forest.

He hadn't gone very far, though, when he suddenly got scared. It would be horrible to go through the forest on his own. And it would be even more horrible to be at Beaver Towers all by himself.

He was just about to turn round when he heard a rustling noise in the leaves behind him.

'I'm coming with you,' Nick said, taking hold of Baby B's paw.

'Hooray!' Baby B said.

'It's best when you've got someone to be with you, isn't it?' Nick said.

'Yes,' Baby B said. 'Yes, it is.'

The two friends hurried on towards Beaver Towers.

CHAPTER FIFTEEN

Baby B and Nick peered out from their hiding place in some bushes just outside Beaver Towers.

Lights were shining from all the windows in the castle and animals were filing across the drawbridge into the courtyard. Soon everybody was inside and the drawbridge was empty. Only a buzz of excited chatter could be heard from the courtyard.

'Come on,' whispered Baby B. 'Let's go and see what's happening.'

They crept out from the bushes and tiptoed across the wooden drawbridge. They hid in the shadows of the archway and peeped into the courtyard.

All the animals of the island were there, crowded round the steps leading to the main door.

Suddenly, the door opened and a hush fell over the crowd. Retsnom hopped out of the Great Hall and stood on the top step. He glared down at the animals with his glittering eyes. They all bowed their heads as if they were afraid to look at him.

'Who is your master?' screamed the raven, and his croaky voice echoed round the courtyard.

'Retsnom! Retsnom!' the animals shouted.

'Yes, for the moment I am your master. I have spoken inside your heads and you are mine. But I serve a greater master and when he comes here, he will be your master, too. I speak of . . . the Prince of Darkness!'

The animals all shivered at the sound of this name and they bowed their heads even lower.

'You do well to tremble,' Retsnom croaked. 'He is all-powerful and he shows no mercy to his enemies. For many years he has yearned to rule over this island. His servants, Oyin and Nomed, were sent to win it for him, but they failed. I, Retsnom, will not fail. Soon he will arrive, but before that glorious moment there is work to be done. You are all my loyal followers but there are some creatures of the island who still refuse to bow to me. You, badger! Come up here and tell us the names of these traitors.'

Baby B and Nick gasped as they saw Mrs Badger climb the steps and turn to face the crowd. She opened her mouth to speak but something stopped her. She shook her head as if she was confused.

Retsnom squawked angrily and flew up and dug his claws into her shoulder.

'Speak the names!' he screamed.

'Baby B and Nick,' Mrs Badger said.

'And what are they, these two creatures?' Retsnom demanded.

'They are traitors,' Mrs Badger said.

She said the words but tears were filling her eyes and Baby B and Nick knew that deep down she must still love them.

'Yes, traitors,' Retsnom shrilled. 'They are the ones who killed the trees. They are the ones who cursed the water and made it go bad. They are your enemies and you must hunt them down. What are their names?'

'Baby B and Nick!' the crowd chanted. 'Baby B and Nick!'

'And what must you do?' Retsnom demanded.

'Hunt them down!' the crowd howled. 'Hunt them down!'

Poor Mrs Badger was still standing on the top step. She was saying everything that the others were saying but she was shaking her head as if she didn't believe it and tears were running down her cheeks.

Retsnom saw the tears and flew up again and pecked her cruelly on the side of her face. The poor badger fell to the ground in pain and a line of blood trickled across the black and white fur on her cheek.

'Oh, Mrs Badger!' Baby B cried, stepping forward out of the shadows.

All the animals were so busy chanting that none of them heard Baby B's cry. None of them except a small rabbit with very sharp ears – Rufus Rabbit. He heard the cry and turned just in time to see Nick rush forward and drag Baby B back into the shadows.

At this very moment, Retsnom pulled himself up proudly and spread his wings wide to get everyone to be quiet. Silence fell. And in the silence, Rufus Rabbit pointed to the archway.

'Baby B and Nick! The traitors! There they are!' he piped in his high voice.

All the animals turned and looked at the archway.

For a second Baby B and Nick were frozen to the spot but then they spun round and dashed away across the drawbridge.

'Hunt them down!' screamed Retsnom as he flapped into the air. He soared high above the castle wall and then dived.

Baby B and Nick had just reached the end of the drawbridge when there was a whirring of wings and a flash of black. Retsnom landed in front of them and they both skidded to a stop.

They could hear the animals running across the drawbridge behind them but Baby B and Nick looked only at Retsnom. His cruel beak was open and his eyes were glittering with triumph.

'I've got you!' he hissed.

Strong paws grabbed hold of Baby B and Nick from behind and they were lifted up into the air.

'To the dungeons with them,' Retsnom croaked. 'Lock them in and leave them. Soon they will sleep. And when they sleep I will speak inside their heads and they will obey. Take them away!'

Baby B and Nick were carried down to the dungeon and thrown inside. The big iron door was locked and they were left alone.

CHAPTER SIXTEEN

Baby B wasn't frightened. Baby B wasn't sad. Baby B was angry.

'That Rufus Rabbit!' he growled as he paced up and down in the dungeon. 'That pesky Rufus Rabbit! The next time I see him I'm going to give him a big biff right on the end of his silly twitchy nose. I know he's only a hinfant and Mr Stripe says you must be kind to hinfants, but look what he's done. We're both locked up in this gungeon and it's all his fault!'

Nick didn't say anything. He was frightened and sad. He sat in the corner and wished it could be like the old days when he was one of the Mechanics, polishing with Ann and Mick. How lovely to be out in the open air making Doris's paintwork shine, rather than trapped here in this damp and gloomy prison.

Nick looked round and sighed. The thick metal door was locked. The walls were carved out of solid rock. The one tiny window, high up near the ceiling, had iron bars so close together that even a small hedgehog wouldn't be able to squeeze through.

It was hopeless to think of escape. And Retsnom was right – sooner or later they would have to go to sleep and he would be able to think-talk to them and make them do anything he wanted.

Bit by bit, Baby B calmed down. He stopped grumbling about Rufus Rabbit and looked round the dungeon as if he had only just realized where he was. He shook the door then he banged his paws against it. He tapped the walls and he scratched the rock floor with his claws. He even tried jumping up to reach the window but it was much too high.

'Oh, Nick,' he said. 'What we going to do?'

'I don't know. I can't think. I'm too tired.'

Nick yawned a big yawn and closed his eyes.

'No!' Baby B shouted. 'No, don't go to sleep. Come on, get up. We must do walking up and down.'

He pulled Nick up and they started walking round the dungeon.

They walked and talked.

They walked and sang their song.

They walked and told silly jokes.

Up and down. Round and round. They walked until their paws ached.

'I got to sit down,' Nick puffed.

'Me too,' Baby B said. 'But we mustn't go to sleep. I've got a good idea – I can sit on you.'

'Sit on me! Why?'

'Well, if your prickles stick in me, I can't sleep. And if I squash you, you can' t sleep as well.'

They tried it. But Nick was much too prickly and Baby B was much too squashy so they had to stop.

'We must do walking again,' Baby B said.

'I can't,' Nick groaned. 'I want to sleep.'

'No – we can't. If we sleep Retsnom will get us. We can sit down a little bit but we must sing the song to keep us awake. One, two, three. "Nick is a hedgehog who's prickerly . . .".'

'It's true,' sang Nick feebly.

'He's covered all over so thickerly . . .'

'Like glue.'

They sang the song all the way through and then started again but their singing got slower and slower as their eyes got heavier and heavier. First Nick's eyes closed and a moment later Baby B's head nodded forward and his eyes closed too.

A few minutes after they had fallen asleep there was a flapping of wings and a bird flew into the dungeon.

CHAPTER SEVENTEEN

Baby B could hear a voice calling in his ear.

'Wake up!' the voice was saying.

'Leave me alone, Nick,' he mumbled. 'I'm too sleepy.'

'It's not Nick. Wake up at once or I'll peck you,' said the voice.

Baby B felt a sharp nip on his ear and he jerked awake to find a bird perched on his shoulder.

'Sergeant Robin! How did you get here?'

'Through the window, of course,' chirped the robin, then he flew down and began gently pecking Nick on his nose. The little hedgehog twitched and opened his eyes.

'No more sleeping – it's time to go,' said the robin.

'Have you come to take us to Retsnom?' Baby B

asked, suddenly afraid.

'Retsnom? Take you to that old lump of evil? Of course not. We've come to set you free.'

'Who's we?' Nick asked.

'Me and Ann – she's getting the key to the door. She'll be here in a minute.'

'But why aren't you hippotrized like everybody else?' Baby B asked.

'I've been away, visiting some friends on another island. And Ann was so busy polishing Doris every night that she was never asleep when Retsnom did his think-talking.'

There was a clicking noise as a key turned in the lock. A moment later the dungeon door swung open and there was Ann standing on a chair.

'I couldn't reach the lock,' she explained. 'I'm all puffed out from pushing the chair. Come on, no time to lose. Nearly everyone's asleep but Retsnom has left some animals on guard so we'll have to be careful.'

'I'll meet you outside,' chirped Sergeant Robin as he flew out of the window.

Ann jumped down from the chair and started climbing the stairs. Baby B and Nick ran out of the dungeon and followed her.

At the top of the stairs, Ann stopped and they all peered along the corridor. In the flickering light from the flaming torches on the wall, they could see a large rabbit who had been left on guard. It was Maxi, the laziest rabbit on the island, so they weren't surprised to see that he was leaning against the wall, asleep.

They held their breath and began to tiptoe along the corridor towards him. As they got closer, they could hear Maxi's gentle snoring and they could see his whiskers twitching in his sleep. Just as they passed him, he began to slide down the wall.

They froze and watched Maxi slip lower and lower until his bottom bumped on to the floor. He was so deeply asleep, though, that he didn't even open his eyes. He just rolled over and went on snoring. They hurried quietly along the corridor and up the next staircase towards the Great Hall.

The Hall seemed empty. They were just about to run across it when they saw the two badgers, Loco and Chez, standing in the shadows near the main door. It was a good place to stand guard – anybody who took one step into the Hall would be spotted at once. Baby B and the two hedgehogs just had to wait and hope that the badgers would go away or fall asleep.

They waited and waited.

The clock near the stairs chimed four o'clock, then half past, then five o'clock.

Loco and Chez showed no sign of going away and there was no hope of them falling asleep because they chatted to each other all the time.

'It'll be morning soon,' Ann whispered. 'If we stay here much longer we're going to be caught.'

It was true, but what could they do?

They were all busy trying to think of something when there was a tap on the door. The two badgers glanced at each other and then slowly opened the door and looked out into the courtyard.

'Who's there?' called Chez.

There was no reply.

'Must be hearing things,' Loco laughed and they closed the door and started chatting again.

There was another tap, louder this time, and the two badgers sprang to the door and threw it open.

'What's going on?' Chez gasped as they looked out and found no one there.

'Perhaps we ought to go and check in the courtyard,' Loco said in a scared voice. 'You go first.'

'No, you go first,' Chez said, pushing Loco in front of him.

The two badgers went timidly out of the door and down the steps. As soon as they'd gone, Baby B and the two hedgehogs dashed across the Hall to the door. They looked out and saw Loco and Chez busily searching the courtyard. Ann pointed to the car standing near the steps.

'We can hide under Doris,' she whispered.

They waited until Loco and Chez had their backs turned then they scooted down the steps and threw themselves under the car. Hidden behind the wheels, they watched as the badgers reached the far end of the courtyard and began walking back towards the steps. They got nearer and nearer and finally stopped right next to the car.

'What do you think?' they heard Loco ask.

'Brrr! I don't know,' Chez said with a shiver. 'All this talk about the Prince of Darkness coming is giving me the collywobbles. I suggest we go inside, lock the door and don't open it, no matter who knocks.'

'Good idea,' Loco said, and the two badgers hurried up the steps and closed the door behind them.

As soon as they heard the key turn in the lock, Baby B, Nick and Ann crawled out from under Doris and rushed across the courtyard. They sprinted over the drawbridge and along the path towards the forest.

When they reached the cover of the first trees they stopped to look back at the castle. It was dark and silent. No one was following them.

'Thank goodness,' panted Ann. 'I thought we would never get out of there.'

There was a whirr of wings and Sergeant Robin flew down and landed on a branch next to them.

'You wouldn't have got out of there if I hadn't half broken my beak banging on that door,' he said.

'Oh, Sergeant Robin, you was millions clever,' Baby B laughed. 'Silly old Loco and Chez was all scared 'cos they thinked it was the Prince of Darkness.'

'Everybody's scared', Ann explained, 'because

they know that Retsnom has sent a message to that wicked Prince. He's expected to arrive later today. And we've got to find a way to stop him or Beaver Towers will be lost for ever. First of all, though, it's nearly daylight and we need somewhere to hide. Any ideas?'

'We know a millions good place, don't we, Nick? Follow us,' Baby B said.

They set off through the forest and by the time they got to the Manor the sun was beginning to rise. They had just made it in time.

They hurried down the stairs and locked themselves in the safety of the secret cellar.

CHAPTER EIGHTEEN

Philip and Mr Edgar pulled their boat up on to the beach and looked round. They were on a tropical island.

Philip was amazed to see that the trees seemed to be coloured red and blue and yellow and green. Then a man stepped out of the trees on to the beach. He clapped his hands once and there was a burst of noise as hundreds of parrots flew into the air. They winged away across the jungle like a moving rainbow.

'Tabby!' shouted Mr Edgar.

The man came forward and put his arm round the old beaver's shoulder.

'Edgar! Good to see you. I hope you liked my colourful welcome. So, this is the young pupil.'

'Yes. Philip – meet Master Tabriz.'

Philip held out his hand and Master Tabriz gripped it warmly. He was a tall black man with a dazzling smile that lit up his whole face. His dark, laughing eyes looked closely at Philip for a moment, then he nodded as if he liked what he saw.

'Well, my old friend,' Master Tabriz said, turning towards Mr Edgar, 'tell me how things are at dear old Beaver Towers – it's so long since I've been there.'

'Ah, if only I knew, Tabby,' Mr Edgar sighed. 'We've totally lost contact. Young Philip here has been sending out think-talk messages for days but we've had no reply.'

'Perhaps my power isn't strong enough,' Philip suggested.

'No, it's not that,' Master Tabriz said. 'Your power is strong. There must be a problem at the other end – your messages aren't being heard.'

'That's what I'm worried about. We almost went straight home rather than come to see you,' Mr Edgar said.

'No, you did right coming here. If there's any trouble at Beaver Towers, Philip is going to need all the power he can get.'

Master Tabriz put his hand on Philip's shoulder. 'You've learned a lot about the world and about yourself – I can see that. The more you understand things like that, the stronger your power will become. So, are you ready for another lesson?'

Philip nodded.

'Good. Follow me.'

He led the way along a path through the jungle until they came to a large round building in the middle of a clearing.

'My observatory,' Master Tabriz said. 'Let us go inside. I want to show you some wonders and mysteries. The wonders and mysteries of the universe.'

CHAPTER NINETEEN

Now that they were safe in the cellar, Baby B and the hedgehogs realized how hungry they were. They sat down and ate some of the nuts and apples they had picked up on their way to the Manor.

It was a delicious breakfast but after they had eaten it, Baby B and Nick felt more sleepy than ever. Sergeant Robin said he knew a herb that was good for staying awake so they pushed open the secret door and he flew off to try to find some in the forest.

'Why did you do polishing Doris at night, Ann?' Nick asked as they waited for the robin to come back.

'Well, someone had to keep her nice and shiny,' she said, giving Nick a meaningful look. 'You got all stuck-up and proud. Then Mick got all silly about helping Retsnom so he stopped working as well. Honestly, boys are useless!'

'No we're not!' Nick cried.

'Who brought Retsnom to Beaver Towers in the first place? Boys!' said Ann. 'Who got caught and put in the dungeon and had to be rescued by a girl? Boys, that's who!'

'That was Rufus Rabbit's fault – just wait till I get hold of him,' blustered Baby B.

'Yes, well he's a boy too. I told you – they're all useless!'

Baby B and Nick didn't dare say anything else because they actually felt a bit useless, although they would never admit it to Ann. So they just sat there trying to look as if they didn't care what she said.

Luckily Sergeant Robin came back at that moment and there was something else to think about. He flew in with a branch in his beak. Baby B and Nick recognized it at once from their lessons on plants. It was called Somstop and Mr Stripe had taught them it was good for staying awake.

They tore off some of the leaves and ate them. Almost at once they felt less tired and they were ready to listen to the robin's news.

While he'd been flying across the island, he'd seen animals everywhere – in the forest, in the fields, even along the seashore. It was obvious that they were looking for Baby B and Nick and it was also obvious that sooner or later they would come to the Manor.

'Yes, but they can't finding us here,' Baby B said, getting up and checking that the secret door was properly closed. 'We're as safe as anything.'

The others hoped he was right.

They all sat silently waiting as the minutes ticked by.

Once, Nick sneezed and everybody jumped with fright and then glared at him.

'I couldn't helping it,' he said.

'Ssshhh!' the others said.

The minutes ticked by.

Ann was the first to hear it.

She stood up, her eyes wide, and pointed at the ceiling.

Then everyone else heard, too. Someone was moving around upstairs. They could hear the steps going from one room to the next. Then they heard the steps coming down the stairs and along the corridor. They heard someone come into the room and walk across to the fireplace. There was a sniffing noise. Then a long silence. Then the sniffing noise came again.

Someone had caught their scent.

There was the sound of more steps and someone else came into the room.

'Come on, this room is empty,' bleated a voice. It was one of the sheep.

'No, come across here near the fireplace,' bleated

the first sheep. 'I'm sure I can smell something.'

They heard the other sheep come across the room. They heard him take a big sniff.

They held their breath.

There was a big sneeze.

'There's just dust and ashes,' bleated the other sheep. 'It's making me sneeze! Come on, let's go – everyone's waiting for us outside.'

'Oh, all right,' bleated the first sheep.

Their hoof-steps went up the stairs and across the floor above.

There was silence in the house.

'I think they've gone,' Ann whispered after a while.

'I'll go and check,' Sergeant Robin said.

They pushed the secret door open and the robin flew out. A minute later he was back with the news that the house was empty and that the sheep had gone off towards the sea.

'Well,' said Ann, 'before anyone comes here again you'd better think-talk to Mr Edgar and ask him what to do about the Prince of Darkness.'

Baby B and Nick had both been dreading this moment and neither of them knew what to say. Baby B nodded at Nick to start but the little hedgehog shook his head and pointed at Baby B.

Somebody had to explain, so finally Baby B took a big gulp and began to tell the whole story about the silly tricks he'd played and how the think-talking had become weaker and weaker until it had stopped completely.

Baby B had expected Ann to go on about how useless he was, but when he finished she simply sighed and said, 'Oh well, I'll have to help you – perhaps the three of us will be strong enough to get through.'

'But you can't do think-talking,' Nick said.

'I think I can,' Ann replied calmly. 'It only started a few nights ago while I was polishing Doris and I can't control it very well, but . . . well, let's see if I can do it now.'

Ann closed her eyes and wrinkled up her nose as she concentrated.

Baby B and Nick both jumped into the air as a picture of a car and the word 'Doris' exploded inside their heads.

'Ow! You must think-talk quieter than that,' Nick groaned, shaking his head. 'You almost blew my prickles off!'

'There you are! I knew I could do it,' Ann smiled.

'You can! Yippee!' Baby B shouted with joy. 'Quick, let's hold paws and see if we can talk to Grandpa Edgar and Flipip. Oh, wouldn't it be millions good if we could?'

The three of them stood in a circle and held paws. Sergeant Robin perched on the logs and watched as they closed their eyes and concentrated.

At first nothing happened, then suddenly all three of them heard a whooshing sound and then a cry of surprise. There was a moment's silence, then Mr Edgar's voice came inside their heads.

'Drat me, what on earth was that?' they heard Mr Edgar say. Then there was a chuckle. 'By Jove! I can't see you and you're very faint but I'd know those think-voices anywhere. It's Baby B and Nick! And about time, you young scamps. I've been as worried as a snowman in a heatwave about you.'

Mr Edgar laughed again, then there was a pause.

'Wait a bit,' he said. 'There's someone else there too. Well, blow me down! Is that Ann?'

'Yes,' said Ann shyly.

'Bravo, lass! You can think-talk! I bet you've been working hard on Doris, eh? Keeping going on your own. Doing your duty without thinking about a reward. That's the ticket. So, you've learned it because you've earned it. Topping! Absolutely topping! Now then, enough chitter-chatter from me – I want to hear what you've got to say.'

So they told him.

CHAPTER TWENTY

One minute Philip had been in Master Tabriz's observatory looking up at the stars through a telescope, and now here he was floating in space looking down at the Earth.

It had all started when Philip had been slowly moving the telescope across the sky. The stars were scattered so thickly that they looked like a glowing cloud of dust against the blackness of space.

'There are so many!' he had gasped.

'Yes, so many,' Master Tabriz had chuckled. 'Many, many millions – and yet they all add up to one.'

'What do you mean?' Philip had asked.

'One universe. You can see it as millions of stars and planets and moons or you can see it as one universe. It's the same with everything. When you look at the sea, are you looking at millions of drops of water or at one sea? When you look at a drop of water, are you looking at millions of atoms of hydrogen and oxygen or at one drop of water? When you look at the Earth, do you see many countries or one planet? All of these things are both many and one at the same time. It just depends on how you see it. Look!'

On that word 'Look', Philip had found himself up here looking down at the beautiful blue and white planet where he lived. And it was true – from up here it was impossible to see cities or countries or continents or the different seas and oceans. From up here it was one planet.

Master Tabriz's voice was still echoing in his head with that word, 'Look!' And now he was rushing back towards the Earth at an incredible speed. The planet was growing larger and larger. Already he could make out the continents set in the blue of the oceans. There was Africa. And there was Europe. Now he could even see the shape of different countries – Italy, Spain, France. He had seen the one, now he was seeing the many.

As he shot closer and closer to the Earth, an enormous curl of cloud billowed up to meet him. And now he was in the cloud, lost in a grey mist made up of many droplets of water.

Master Tabriz's voice still echoed, 'Look!'

And as Philip looked, the droplets were merging and melting together to make larger droplets that started to fall as rain. And he was falling with the rain.

He was inside a drop of rain, looking out through the liquid walls, as it tumbled down from an enormous height. One drop of rain, surrounded by millions of other drops.

And inside the drop of rain, he found himself wrapped in a green fog as two gases swirled and twined together. And he knew that it must be hydrogen and oxygen mixing to form water.

The word 'Look!' still echoed in his head, so he looked. And he saw that each gas was made up of millions of atoms dancing together. And while his drop of rain continued to fall towards the Earth, he fell towards one of the atoms.

He burst through the fizzing surface of the atom and found himself in a silent emptiness so huge that it was like being back in outer space. But instead of looking down at the Earth, he was looking across a vast distance towards a tiny speck at the centre of the atom. A speck of energy that crackled and sparkled and dazzled like the sun.

At the heart of the speck was nothing. And from this nothing the crackling and the sparkling and the dazzling flashed into being.

And he stayed there a long time watching the miracle happen. The miracle of creation, as nothing became something.

Then he felt himself rising again, being drawn back out of the atom. Back through the fizzing surface and into the green fog of the gases.

Then the green swirl of the gases parted and he was looking out of the clear watery walls of the raindrop again. One of millions of raindrops falling towards the Earth. And he could see where his raindrop and all the others around him were heading. The sea lay below them.

'Look!' echoed Master Tabriz's voice.

There was a hiss as his raindrop hit the surface of the sea. And as the hiss faded away he felt the smooth round walls of the raindrop melt. The water rushed out and the sea rushed in and then there was no difference.

He was a drop of water and he was the sea. He was one of the many, and he was part of the one. And he moved in one place far out at sea, yet he was also the wave that curled and crashed against the land hundreds of miles away.

Then a voice was calling to him. Not Master Tabriz's voice. Mr Edgar's voice.

'Philip, come back! Philip, come back!' it called.

He opened his eyes and he was back in the observatory. Master Tabriz was standing by the telescope and Mr Edgar was walking up and down with a worried look on his old grey face.

CHAPTER TWENTY-ONE

'There's danger at Beaver Towers,' Mr Edgar said. 'Terrible danger.'

Philip felt his heart beating faster and faster as Mr Edgar told him what Baby B and the others had managed to say before their think-talking had faded away.

'The poor young scamps were so scared that they were all think-talking at once. And their signal was getting weaker every second. I had a high old time trying to make sense of it all. They kept going on about some bird who has hypnotized all the animals on the island. Now what was the dratted name of the rotter? Ah yes, Retsnom, that's it.'

'Retsnom?' Master Tabriz said. 'I know that name. He's one of the helpers of the Prince of Darkness. But Retsnom isn't a bird. Change the letters of his name around and you'll soon see what he really is – a monster. A huge, horrible, slimy, slug-like monster. He must be in disguise.'

'Well, whatever he is, he's got Beaver Towers in his power,' said Mr Edgar. 'And the Prince of Darkness is on his way there to take control. We'll never get back there in time.'

'In that case, your grandson and his friends will have to do battle on their own,' Master Tabriz said calmly.

'But they're just three young animals – how can they do it? Baby B can't even think-talk properly any more. You know what they say, 'Misuse it and you'll lose it' – well, he's lost it.'

'What do you want them to do, then?' Master Tabriz asked, looking at Mr Edgar. 'Lie down and wait for the Prince of Darkness to take them into his power? Even young animals can show love and courage. And remember, love and courage can work miracles.'

'By Jove! You're right, Tabby!' Mr Edgar said, slapping Master Tabriz on the back. 'Never say die, eh? That's the stuff! Come on, young Philip – show us how much you've learned. Get that power of yours working. See if you can contact our little heroes and tell them what they've got to do.'

Philip closed his eyes. He could feel the power bubbling up inside him, stronger than ever. There was a huge surge inside his head and he sent his thoughts spinning out towards the Manor.

In a flash he was there, looking at Baby B, Nick and Ann sitting on the floor of the cellar. They were holding paws, still trying to think-talk to Mr Edgar and they all jumped with surprise when he spoke to them.

'Flipip!' Baby B shouted with joy when he got over his shock. 'Where are you?'

'I'm with Mr Edgar in Master Tabriz's observatory – it's a very long way away, I'm afraid.'

'I wish you was here, Flipip, then you could biff smelly old Retsnom and bonk him on the head.'

'I wish I were there, too,' Philip chuckled. 'Mr Edgar and I will be back as soon as we can but we won't be there in time to help you. You're going to have to deal with Retsnom on your own.'

'We can help,' Ann and Nick said.

'So can I,' chirped Sergeant Robin, flying down from his perch on the logs and landing on Baby B's shoulder.

'That's right,' Philip said. 'You must all help each other. Evil creatures hate it when friends stick together and look after each other.'

'What must we have to do, Flipip?' Baby B asked.

'First you must tell the other animals the truth about Retsnom. He's not really a bird, he's a monster. When they stop believing in him he won't be able to hypnotize them.'

'But they won't listen to me.'

'Then you must go to Beaver Towers and think-talk to them.'

'I can't,' Baby B said sadly. 'I can't do proper think-talking now. I losed it 'cos I mischewed it.'

'Listen, Baby B, it's very important. You've *got* to do it!' Philip urged. 'I can think-talk to you and help you. But you've got to be brave and go to the castle.'

'But I'm *not* brave,' Baby B suddenly wailed as he thought about the dangers ahead.

'Of course you are, Baby B,' Philip said and he sent out the warmest, most loving thoughts he could towards his friend. 'You're the bravest little beaver I've ever met.'

'Am I really?' Baby B asked, with a shy smile.

'Yes, really.'

'Well, you're the bestest human beak I ever met, Flipip,' Baby B said.

'Thank you.'

'And Nick's the bestest Nick I ever met, and Ann's the bestest Ann, and Sergeant Robin is the bestest Sergeant Robin,' Baby B said. Then he added, 'And Retsnom is the smelliest of all smellies!'

Everybody laughed, and the laughter seemed to fill Baby B with courage because he stood up and said, 'And I'm going to Beaver Towers and I'm going to biff him to make him go away. Paws up, anybody who wants to help.'

Nick and Ann quickly raised a paw and Sergeant

Robin lifted the tip of his wing.

'Hooray!' cried Baby B. 'Come on, let's go!'

'Good luck!' Philip said. 'And remember, I'll be there if you need my help.'

He watched as they ran up the steps, pushed open the small stone door, and rushed out of the cellar. He let the picture of the Manor flicker and fade away.

He opened his eyes and found himself back in the observatory with Mr Edgar and Master Tabriz.

Nobody said anything, but in the silence he knew they were all thinking the same thing. Baby B and his friends had gone charging off bravely but they were only small animals and they were facing a mighty force of evil.

They had love and courage on their side but if they failed, they would be crushed. And Beaver Towers would be lost for ever.

CHAPTER TWENTY-TWO

Baby B and the two hedgehogs set off along the path and Sergeant Robin went winging away across the forest to check for danger.

As the sun dipped below the trees there was a cool dampness in the air and a mist began to rise from the ground. Bushes loomed out of the mist like ghosts and the three friends walked closer together and looked round anxiously.

Wings fluttered above them and they all ducked, thinking it was Retsnom, but it was Sergeant Robin. He told them that the forest was all clear and that he had flown over the castle and seen everyone standing completely still in the courtyard.

'They is waiting for the Prince of Darkness,' Baby B said with a shiver. He wanted to turn right round and go back to the safety of the Manor but he smiled at the others and pretended he wasn't scared. 'Come on, there's nobody in the forest so we can do running.'

They ran along the misty forest path until they came in sight of the castle, then they hid under some bracken to decide what to do next. The sun went down and night fell as they tried to think of a plan.

'We've got to tell everyone about Retsnom,' Ann said.

'But we can't go in the courtyard or they will catch us,' Nick pointed out.

'I've got a good idea,' Baby B said. 'We go in the secret tunnel to the castle. Then we climb out of a window near the courtyard and we will be too very high to be catched.'

They all agreed that it was a good plan so they crept along the edge of the forest until they came to the steps that led to the tunnel. They parted the ferns and started down the steps, then stopped in surprise – the entrance to the tunnel was blocked by a row of wooden stakes.

'Retsnom must have thinked we might come in here,' Baby B groaned.

'We'll have to go across the drawbridge then,' Ann said.

'No, there will be guards waiting for us – probably that pesky Rufus Rabbit,' Baby B said, then he took a good look at the stakes. 'It will take me millions long but I can make a hole in the wood.'

It did take a long time – hours and hours – while Ann and Nick sat on the steps and watched Baby B gnawing at the wooden posts. Sometimes they helped by clearing away some of the wood chippings but it was Baby B who did all the hard work.

Sergeant Robin kept flying off to see what was happening in the courtyard but he always came back with the same report – there was no sign of Retsnom and the animals were still all rooted to the spot, waiting.

'Finished!' Baby B said at last. 'Phew, my teeth don't half feel tired.'

They patted him on the back for all the hard work he'd done, then they squeezed through the hole he had made.

It was so dark in the tunnel that Sergeant Robin couldn't fly so he perched on Baby B's shoulder. They moved forward slowly, feeling the ground in front of them in case Retsnom had left any traps for them. The walls were wet and slimy and the constant drip-drip of water echoed along the tunnel sounding horribly like footsteps following them.

They were glad when they felt the ground slope upwards and they came to the steps that led up to the library. They climbed up the twisty, rock staircase and reached the secret door. Baby B leaned forward to push it open but Nick tugged at his dungarees to stop him.

'S'posing Retsnom's in the library,' the little hedgehog whispered.

Too late.

Baby B had already put his weight against the door and it had started to swing open.

CHAPTER TWENTY-THREE

The library was empty.

They dashed across the room to the other door and peered up and down the corridor – no one. They tiptoed along the corridor and down the stairs to the next level. From here, the windows looked out directly on to the courtyard.

Baby B opened one of the windows and Sergeant Robin flew out across the courtyard and landed on the castle wall opposite. Ann and Nick climbed out on to the ledge, then Baby B heaved himself up and joined them outside.

The ledge was quite wide but it was very high up and Baby B felt a bit dizzy when he looked down. He moved slowly along the ledge, followed by Nick and Ann, until they were right above the main door to the castle.

The only movement below was from the flickering flames of the torches that lit up the courtyard. All the animals were standing as still as statues, staring at the door. They were in a deep trance.

'I'm going to shout to wake them up,' Baby B said.

'But s'posing Retsnom hears you and comes and gets us,' Nick whispered with a shiver.

'Oh yes,' Baby B said. 'I know – let's try and think-talk to them.'

He took hold of Ann's paw and she held on to Nick's paw. They closed their eyes and concentrated.

'Don't listen to Retsnom,' Baby B thought, as hard as he could. 'Mr Edgar and Flipip is coming back but you must have to stop being hippotrized by smelly Retsnom. Lift your paw or your hoof if you can hear me.'

He opened his eyes. None of the animals had moved; they were still staring at the door.

'They can't hear you,' Ann said. 'Try again.'

They closed their eyes and squeezed their paws tighter while Baby B tried even harder to think-talk to the animals below. He thought and thought but still they didn't move.

Baby B was just about to try for a third time, when there was the sound of the door opening below. Light spilled out from the open door on to the top of the steps and Retsnom came hopping out of the castle.

He stood on the top step and gave three loud croaks.

The animals blinked and stirred as they came out of the trance. Then they caught sight of the big black bird with the light shining on him and they began clapping and cheering.

Rufus Rabbit ran to the front of the crowd and began chanting, 'Retsnom! Retsnom!' All the animals joined in the chant and soon the courtyard echoed with his name.

The raven stood for a while, his eyes glittering with pride, then he opened his wings wide. At once, the animals fell silent.

'I have great news,' Retsnom croaked. 'The Prince of Darkness is coming. At this very moment he is on his way. He will be here by dawn. Soon you will be his slaves and you will obey his every word. Who do you love?'

'The Prince of Darkness!' the animals cried.

'Who do you love?' Retsnom croaked again.

'The Prince of Darkness!'

It was so terrible to see all the animals of the island calling out this dreadful name that Baby B forgot what he was doing. He leaned over the edge of the ledge and shouted out loud, 'No! No! You don't love the Prince of Darkness. He's evil!'

A silence fell over the courtyard. Some of the animals looked about them, puzzled, as if they had heard something but didn't know where it was coming from.

'I'm up here!' Baby B shouted again. 'It's me, Baby B. Don't listen to Retsnom! He's your henemy.'

There was a gasp from the animals and they all looked up. None of them seemed to know what to do. Then Rufus Rabbit ran up the steps shouting, 'The traitors! It's the traitors!'

There was a terrible squawk from Retsnom and he beat his ragged wings and flew into the air.

He rose high above the courtyard and looked down. Baby B, Nick and Ann pressed back into the shadows against the wall, hoping to hide. But it was no use. Retsnom saw them at once and dived to attack.

Baby B cringed low and closed his eyes as the bird plunged towards them. He felt wing-tips brush across his back then he heard two little screams. When he opened his eyes he saw Retsnom flying away with Nick clutched in one claw and Ann in the other.

For one awful moment Baby B thought that the evil bird was going to let them drop to their death in the courtyard. Instead, he swooped low and put them down next to Loco and Chez.

'Guard them! I will deal with them later,' Retsnom croaked to the two badgers, then he hopped round and looked up towards Baby B. 'But first, I will kill that stupid little beaver up there.'

Just then, Baby B heard a noise from the window and he glanced round to see Rufus Rabbit scrambling out on to the ledge.

'It's the traitor,' squeaked Rufus and he began to run along the ledge towards Baby B.

The young rabbit had only taken a few steps, though, when he happened to glance down and see how high up he was. It was such a shock for him that his front paws got all tangled up with each other and he tripped. He tumbled flat on his face and rolled off the ledge.

At the last moment he managed to grab hold of the edge with one paw. His little claws dug into the stone and he hung there, high above the courtyard. His weight was too much, though, and his claws suddenly slipped and slid nearer the edge before he managed to dig them in again.

'Help!' Rufus screamed to Baby B. 'Help!'

For just one second Baby B thought, 'Serve him right. Let the pesky little thing fall.'

But even before he had finished thinking it, he had darted forward and grabbed the little rabbit's paw. He pulled him up and set him down safely on the ledge.

Rufus Rabbit's big eyes filled with tears and he started to tremble from head to foot.

'Don't cry, silly billy,' Baby B said gently. 'You're safe now.'

There was a strange tingling inside Baby B's head and his brain was suddenly filled with words.

'Fall down . . . Mummy . . . fall . . . Baby B . . . Mr Retsnom . . . Mummy . . . traitor . . . hurt me . . . friend . . .'

Baby B realized he was hearing the jumble of scared thoughts that were racing round in Rufus Rabbit's head. That must mean that his think-talking powers had started to come back.

There was a loud flapping noise and Baby B spun round to see Retsnom flying towards them.

Rufus Rabbit saw him too. He gave a squeak of fear and covered his eyes with his paws. Baby B pushed the little rabbit back against the wall and stood in front of him.

Retsnom was coming. His cruel beak was open and his razor-sharp claws were raised.

There was a blur of red as something dived down from the sky.

It was Sergeant Robin.

The small bird pounced on Retsnom, pecked him on the head, and went whizzing away with a couple of black feathers in his beak. The raven let out a croak of anger and gave chase.

The brave little robin had done it to save Baby B, but now he was the one in danger. Retsnom was nearly on him. The huge raven opened his beak, ready to snatch him out of the air and crush him. But the robin knew exactly what he was doing.

Just as Retsnom swooped down on him, Sergeant Robin dodged to the side and dived towards the courtyard wall. He darted into a crack between two stones in the wall and hid. The hole was far too small for the big bird to follow so the robin was safe.

Retsnom let out an angry squawk, wheeled round in the air, and started back towards Baby B.

This time Sergeant Robin wouldn't be able to save him. This time Retsnom's pointed claws would grab him and hurl him down into the courtyard.

Baby B shivered and tears started to fill his eyes.

Then suddenly he heard Philip calling to him inside his head.

'Come on, Baby B – don't be afraid. I'm here with you. Remember what I told you. Retsnom isn't a real bird at all. He just looks like a bird because of magic. Laugh at him. Trick him into showing you what he really is.'

'I can't,' Baby B cried. 'I'm too little. I can't.'

'Yes, you can!' he heard Philip say. 'You rescued Rufus – that's why your think-talking has come back. Now you must be just as brave and trick Retsnom. Laugh at him. Come on. It's your last chance. Do it now!'

As Retsnom flew towards him, Baby B felt Philip's power filling him. He opened his mouth and shouted with all his might.

'Yoo-hoo! Smelly Retsnom,' he yelled. 'I'm not scared of you. You're just a silly old bird.'

Baby B saw the look of surprise in Retsnom's eyes and it gave him the courage to go on. He took a deep breath and started singing a silly song that he'd learned in the playground at school.

> 'Hee-hee, cup of tea!
> You couldn't scare a flea!'

Retsnom let out a scream of rage.

'Not scared of a silly old bird, eh?' he squawked. 'Well then, take a look at what I'm really like.'

Baby B gasped as he saw Retsnom begin to change. The body grew larger and larger and the glossy black feathers began to melt into wet skin. In an instant, the raven had turned back into his real shape.

He was a huge, glistening slug with green slime oozing from his hideous mouth.

The sight was so awful that Baby B had to close his eyes, but he could still hear the monster's horrible voice.

'You see!' he heard Retsnom hiss. 'They don't call me Retsnom the Monster for nothing. And now I . . . Oh no! Help!'

There was a terrible scream and Baby B opened his eyes in time to see the monster falling towards the courtyard.

Philip's trick had worked!

Without his bird-disguise to keep him in the air, Retsnom was crashing back to the earth.

There was a dreadful squelching sound as Retsnom hit the ground and his flabby body split open. He twitched once, then lay still.

He was dead.

CHAPTER TWENTY-FOUR

For a moment there was total silence in the courtyard.

Then suddenly all the animals began shaking their heads and yawning and rubbing their eyes and stretching their arms up in the air. It looked just as if they were waking up after a long sleep.

Baby B felt a movement behind him and Rufus Rabbit pushed past him.

'Up here!' shouted the little rabbit. 'He's up here!'

Oh no! Did Rufus Rabbit still think he was a traitor? Was he still under Retsnom's power? If he was, then all the other animals would be too.

'Baby B is up here,' shouted Rufus again. 'He's the one who killed Retsnom.'

The little rabbit grabbed hold of Baby B's paw and held it up in the air.

'Three cheers for Baby B!' shouted Rufus. 'Hip hip . . .'

'Hooray!'

The courtyard echoed with the cheers of each and every one of the animals and Baby B knew they were his friends again.

'Yippee!' he shouted. 'You've stopped being hippotrized!'

Everyone began laughing and hugging each other and jumping around with happiness.

Rufus Rabbit got so excited jumping up and down that he nearly fell off the ledge again, so Baby B took hold of him and led him back inside. They ran through the castle and down into the courtyard.

Ann and Nick were waiting for Baby B by the steps and all the animals started cheering again when they saw the three young heroes together. Baby B's mother and father ran up and kissed him and hugged him and it was wonderful to feel how much they loved him.

'Oh, Baby B,' said Mrs Badger, coming up to him. 'Bless my soul, I just don't know what to say. To think that I called you a traitor and . . . oh dear, it's so terrible . . .'

She pulled a hanky from her apron and burst into tears.

'We're sorry too,' called Loco and Chez.

'So am I,' said Mick, giving Ann and Nick a little hedgehoggy kiss on their snouts.

'We're all sorry,' Mr Stripe said. 'That wretched Retsnom made us all lose our heads.'

'You see, Mrs Badger,' Baby B said, putting his arms round her neck. 'You couldn't helping it. You just losted your head.'

Mrs Badger had to chuckle. She wiped the tears from her eyes and gave Baby B a big hug.

At that very moment, a flash of lightning zigzagged across the sky and a crash of thunder shook the courtyard.

'The Prince of Darkness!' Mr Stripe shouted. 'We've forgotten all about him. Quick!'

Mr Stripe ran up the steps to the top of the castle wall and everyone followed. They looked out across the forest towards the sea.

The first glow of day was touching the horizon but the sky was still very dark.

Then they saw it.

A huge cloud, darker than the night, was racing towards the island. Lightning flashed from its base and thunder boomed from its heart.

The cloud sped closer and they began to feel the wind that howled around it. The trees of the forest bent and swayed. Millions of leaves were ripped from their branches and sent swirling up into the sky.

Lightning lit up the cloud again and the animals saw the face. One moment there was just boiling, twisting vapour, the next moment it was the face of the beast. A wild, terrible beast.

The Prince of Darkness.

His red serpent-eyes opened and the animals stepped back in terror.

Then they heard Mr Stripe's voice above the roar of the storm.

'Hold paws!' he cried. 'Hold paws! He thinks we are still in Retsnom's power. He thinks we are scared and that we hate each other. Show him that he is the one we hate. Hold paws and show him!'

Mr Stripe grabbed hold of Mrs Badger's paw. She took took hold of Nick's paw. Nick took hold of Baby B's paw. Baby B took hold of Rufus Rabbit's paw.

All the way down the line, the animals took each other's paws and held them up.

The red serpent-eyes blinked in shock.

Those cruel eyes grew wide again and a dreadful roar rolled out of the cloud.

But the animals stood firm.

No one ran away. They held paws and faced the beast.

The eyes snapped shut.

The face faded away.

The wind stopped howling.

The first ray of the morning sun shot up into the sky and pierced through the cloud. Bright golden light shone through the centre of the shadowy mists, melting it to nothing.

The animals stood there, paw in paw, until the night had gone and Beaver Towers was bathed in warm sunlight.

CHAPTER TWENTY-FIVE

Two weeks later, Baby B set out from Beaver Towers for a walk.

The air was cool and crisp. Winter was coming. There was already snow on the top of the tallest mountain. Soon there would be all the fun of snow-balls and sliding and telling stories round the fire at night.

He strolled through the forest. The trees were bare since the storm but they were all healthy, even the ones that Retsnom had made ill. He stopped at the first stream he came to and he took a sip of the water. Sweet and clean again – like the water in the wells.

The bubbling stream looked so inviting that Baby B couldn't resist dipping his paws in it. Then it seemed like a good idea to see how big a splash he could make by slapping the water with his tail. It was a very big splash indeed. In fact it was so big that the legs of his dungarees were soaking wet.

After that, there didn't seem much point in trying to stay dry so he jumped straight into the stream and started swimming.

The stream led to the River Busy and the river flowed right out to the sea, so he kept on swimming until he came to the salty waves. He swam along the shore, racing with shoals of fish and surfing in the waves.

Then he ran ashore and started to search for treasure in the sand. When he couldn't stuff any more coloured pebbles and shells into the bulging pockets of his dungarees, he sat down on a rock and watched the waves.

He was still watching them an hour later when he saw a sail in the distance. He stood up to get a better view. The little boat was skimming fast across the waves and as it got closer Baby B let out a big shout of joy.

'Grandpa! Flipip!'

Mr Edgar and Philip stood up and waved. Then, as soon as the boat glided gently on to the sand, they jumped ashore and took turns in hugging the little beaver.

'Drat me! You're a sight for sore eyes, you little scamp!' Mr Edgar said. 'Now tell us what's been going on here while we've been away.'

Philip lifted Baby B up on to his shoulders and

the little beaver started his story as they walked along. His excited voice rang out among the trees as they crossed the forest and he was still chattering away when they reached the castle.

'By Jove! It sounds as if we're lucky to find the old place still standing,' Mr Edgar said as they crossed the drawbridge. 'Oh, it's so good to be home.'

Mrs Badger was the first to see them arrive and her cries of joy brought everyone running to the courtyard.

In no time at all a 'Welcome Home' party had started in the Great Hall. There was singing and dancing and plenty of delicious food. And everybody laughed and had such good fun that the party was still going on when night-time came.

Baby B was allowed to stay up late, but his eyes got sleepier and sleepier and at last he asked Philip to take him upstairs to bed. He undressed quickly and popped under the covers and Philip sat on the bed and read to him.

They had just finished the story when Mr Edgar came into the room. He kissed Baby B on the top of his head and made sure he was well tucked-up.

'Well, you young rascal,' Mr Edgar said, 'You certainly got yourself in a bit of a pickle, didn't you? But all's well that ends well.'

'Grandpa . . . ' Baby B said.

'What is it, lad?'

'Is you and Flipip going away again?'

'Got no plans to leave, no,' Mr Edgar said. 'Our mission was a success and young Philip has learned enough for the moment.'

'Good,' Baby B said. 'I like it bestest when you are the ones who have to be growed up and riskonstable. I just want to be Baby B like before.'

'Had a few too many adventures for the moment, have you?' Mr Edgar said, stroking his grandson's cheek.

Baby B nodded.

'Well, don't worry your noddle. You're quite safe. Philip and I can look after things now.'

Baby B smiled and snuggled down to sleep. Mr Edgar and Philip got up and went to the door.

'You've left my light on,' Baby B called.

'I thought you might want it,' Philip said.

'Crumbs, Flipip!' Baby B said, sitting up in bed. 'I'm not a hinfant!'

He leaned over, blew out the night light, and then snuggled back down under the covers.

'Night, night, young 'un,' Mr Edgar said, going out of the door.

'Night, Grandpa. Night, Flipip.'

'Night, Baby B,' said Philip. 'Sleep tight.'

'I will,' Baby B said sleepily.

And he did.